A MESSAGE FROM CHICKEN HOUSE

I have always found friends in books: fictional characters were the best company for a lonely little boy beset by illness and big sisters! So it was with huge enthusiasm that I read Lucy Strange's haunting tale of a terrific girl called Henry who draws inspiration, wonder and strength from books. Henry's bravery in the face of terrible risks kept me racing to the very last page of this beautiful and mesmerizing novel. Set over a long, dreamy summer, *The Secret of Nightingale Wood* already enchants like a true classic.

BARRY CUNNINGHAM
Publisher
Chicken House

Lucy Strange

The Secret of Nightingale Wood

2 Palmer Street, Frome, Somerset BA11 1DS
www.chickenhousebooks.com

Text © Lucy Strange 2016

First published in Great Britain in 2016
Chicken House
2 Palmer Street
Frome, Somerset BA11 1DS
United Kingdom
www.chickenhousebooks.com

Cover and interior design by Helen Crawford-White
Typeset by Dorchester Typesetting Group Ltd
Printed and bound in Great Britain by CPI Group (UK) Ltd, Croydon CR0 4YY

The paper used in this Chicken House book is made from
wood grown in sustainable forests.

3 5 7 9 10 8 6 4

British Library Cataloguing in Publication data available.

PB ISBN 978-1-910655-03-0
eISBN 978-1-910655-63-4

'Do I wake or sleep?'

John Keats, *Ode to a Nightingale*

For my parents, Mary and Rick Strange

'Life is a splendid gift – there is nothing small about it.'
Florence Nightingale

I

We stood together, looking up at the new house – Father, Mama, Nanny Jane, Piglet and me. It was large and old, almost falling down in places, with gently bulging walls and a steep, tiled roof that was etched with lichen. The sign on the gatepost read HOPE HOUSE.

'It's a fresh start,' Father said.

Mama didn't say anything. She just stared at our strange new home, and then turned to stare at Father.

'Come on, Piglet,' I whispered to the baby. 'Let's have a look around.'

I clutched her tightly to my chest and walked around the side of the house, towards the long garden and the wilderness of woodland that lay beyond.

'Don't be long,' Nanny Jane called after me. 'Be

back for tea in twenty minutes please, Henry.'

I had always been Henry, even though my full name was Henrietta Georgina Abbott. Maybe my parents had wanted two boys. Now that my brother Robert had gone, they had two girls. Just me and Piglet.

Piglet wasn't the baby's real name either, of course. She had arrived during that terrible time last summer. Mama wouldn't discuss what to call her, so Father had registered her as Roberta Abbott – a horrible mistake, but it was too late now. No one could bear to call her Roberta, so we called her Piglet because, well, she looked a lot like a baby pig. I liked the name because it reminded me of the baby in *Alice's Adventures in Wonderland*.

I felt a lot like Alice that day, exploring a new world in which nothing quite made sense. Piglet and I wandered past a dishevelled herb garden, an overgrown bed of rose bushes and a broken old gazebo, all the way down the length of the lawn to the point at which the garden ended and the forest began.

Beneath the trees it was cool, dark and badgery. It had been a hot summer, and the leaves and twigs beneath my feet were as crisp as kindling. A tangle of overgrown pathways wound away into the darkness of the forest. I stopped and listened, but I could only hear the soft thrum of my own heartbeat and the whisper of Piglet's breathing. She suddenly felt heavy in my arms and I realized she had fallen asleep. I kissed the top of her fluffy round head. 'Funny little Piglet,' I whispered.

I stepped forward on to the nearest path, and then stopped. *What if I get lost and can't find my way back?* I thought. *What if the shadows of the forest swallow me up?* The branches above shivered strangely, and then, quite suddenly, I could smell smoke.

Smoke. That thick, bitter smell that filled my nightmares.

I turned and stumbled out of the trees, gripping the baby so tightly that she jolted awake and cried out. I patted her and tried to laugh, pretending my clumsy panic had just been a game. 'It's all right,' I said. She whimpered, unconvinced.

I looked back into the forest and saw a wraith of smoke drifting towards me through the trees.

The sunlit leaves trembled with secrets.

That evening, I helped bath Piglet, and then I read to her as she fussed in her cot, squirming and babbling. She liked being read to, or at least she liked trying to chew the corners of the book. I stroked her little turned-up nose with my fingertip, and by the time I got to the final verse of *The Owl and the Pussycat*, her eyes were starting to close.

They dined on mince, and slices of quince,
Which they ate with a runcible spoon;
And hand in hand, on the edge of the sand,
They danced by the light of the moon . . .

'Night night, Piglet,' I said, and tucked the blanket around her plump middle. And then I said, 'Runcible,' because it was a lovely word and I didn't know if it was real or not. I closed the nursery door softly behind me and went downstairs for supper.

Nanny Jane and I sat at the dining table for nearly ten minutes before Father joined us. We heard his raised voice upstairs, and then a door slammed shut. The old house shook and I half expected to hear Piglet's cries drifting down the stairs, but she didn't wake up.

Nanny Jane stirred her cooling soup and waited patiently – a vision of control, with her immaculate white apron and her hair pulled back into a perfect blonde bun. I asked her if she knew whether or not 'runcible' was a real word and she said she wasn't sure. I said I would ask Father.

'Not this evening, Henry,' she said.

When Father sat down he started eating his tepid soup immediately, without a word to either of us.

'Will Mama be coming down for supper?' I asked.

Nanny Jane shot me one of her looks.

Father swallowed his soup, touched his mouth with his napkin, and took a deep breath. 'I don't think so, Henry,' he said. 'Your mother is very tired.'

He suddenly looked very tired too and his eyes seemed to sparkle unnaturally, as if they had filled with tears. He looked down and rubbed his forehead.

I tried to think of something else to say.

'I think there might be someone in the woods,' I said. 'When I was looking around this afternoon, I thought I could smell smoke . . .'

Father pushed his chair away from the table and stood up. 'It has been a long day for all of us . . . And I'm not that hungry after all.'

He walked to the door.

'Perhaps give the stories a miss tonight,' he said, without looking back. 'You're too old for fairy tales now, Henry.'

I assumed Father had gone to bed, but I was wrong. After supper, I followed the smell of his pipe smoke to a study at the front of the house, just off the hallway. Bare wooden bookshelves lined each wall, from the parquet floor up to the high ceiling, so that it felt like an abandoned book shop.

Father had begun to unpack a few boxes, but now he was just sitting in a high-backed armchair beside the empty fireplace, smoking his pipe. He must have heard me come in, but he didn't say anything, so I didn't say anything either.

Books stood in neat piles on the floor, ready to be shelved. I picked up Father's heavy dictionary and flicked hopefully through the pages.

'Runcible' wasn't there.

2

That night I couldn't sleep.

I spent an hour or more sitting on the floor of my bedroom in my nightgown, unpacking my books from the travelling trunk and putting them on the bookshelf. I arranged them alphabetically: Louisa May Alcott, Frances Hodgson Burnett, Lewis Carroll, Charles Dickens . . . Then I took them all off the shelf and started again, this time using the spines to create a rainbow of colour – blue, green, grey, black . . .

I put my book of fairy tales on the bedside table; it didn't live with my other books. My brother Robert had given it to me for my twelfth birthday, very nearly a year ago. It was filled with the most beautiful pictures you could ever imagine – page after page of enchanted forests, underwater cities and royal palaces. The longer you looked at those pictures, the more you would see – there were pictures within the pictures, worlds within worlds.

My new bedroom was at the back of the house, overlooking the garden and the woods beyond. I opened the heavy curtains and stood at the dark window, but all I could see was my own reflection looking back at me.

There were dark circles under my eyes, my hair was a tangled brown mess. A year ago, Mama would have laughed and said, 'You look like you've been dragged through a hedge by a runaway pony, Hen.' She would have pulled me towards her and gently brushed at the bird's nest until my hair shone. She would have kissed me goodnight.

I blinked away the tears, and pulled the curtains together behind me to shut out the light.

The darkness beyond the window was vast and deep, nothing like the hazy grey of London at night. *This sky belongs in my book of fairy tales*, I thought. *An evil queen's black velvet cloak, embroidered with diamonds . . .*

And then I saw the smoke.

It was drifting up in a thin wisp from the shadowy woods. As I squinted at it, I saw a tiny orange light flickering among the trees. A fire. *Someone has lit a fire in our forest.*

My heart clenched like a fist. I thought of all the

dead leaves on the forest floor, the twigs as crisp as kindling. I imagined the fire growing and spreading, leaping up and catching hold of the bone-dry branches above; I saw it tearing through the trees towards Hope House . . .

I stared and stared at the fire until my eyes burned, but it didn't grow or tear or leap. It glowed. It – *twinkled* . . .

I wanted to pretend I hadn't seen it, to put my nightdress on and cuddle down beneath the soft blue blanket with my book of fairy tales, but the brightness of the fire was somehow magical, magnetic, like a faery flame.

Without letting myself think about what I was doing, I put on my boots and dressing gown, and opened the bedroom door.

I stood on the landing and listened for Father's snores, but everything was quiet. I thought I had heard the engine of a motor car earlier, and now, standing there in the darkness and silence, I felt a little jolt of panic – what if everyone had packed up and gone back to London without me? Then came the low, comforting murmur of an adult voice. Father. Perhaps he couldn't sleep either . . .

I made my way down the stairs, sticking to the edge of the staircase near the bannister, where the wood was less likely to bend and creak beneath my feet. I imagined my brother Robert's voice whispering at me from the landing: '*You're supposed to be in bed,* Henrietta . . .' and my heart thudded guiltily. I wondered if Nanny Jane could tell if a child was wearing boots instead of slippers just from the sound of a creaking stair.

I crept through the hallway and into the kitchen. The table was piled with boxes of our things from London. They stood open, as though someone had started unpacking them and had been called away. I saw crystal wine glasses and a pretty dinner service decorated with pink roses. I hadn't seen these things since the Christmas before last, and I didn't think it was likely that they would be used again very soon. Things weren't like that any more in the Abbott family.

The door to the garden was locked. On the wall to the left of the door was a row of hooks, and each hook had a different key hanging from it. One had a little label attached with a loop of garden twine – KITCHEN DOOR. The key grated reluctantly in the lock and the door swung open.

With the faint light of the kitchen behind me, the garden was a dark greeny-grey – like the bottom of the ocean. I could just make out the shipwreck of the old gazebo drifting and creaking somewhere beyond the sprawling herb garden. In front of me there floated a few half-closed white roses; the rosebush itself was almost invisible in the gloom, so the flowers bobbed about like ghostly jellyfish. I found that I was holding my breath, as if I really were underwater. I forced myself to take a big gulp of air, and stepped on to the lawn.

As I walked through the garden, my shadow stretched ahead of me, towards the mysterious forest. It sat there darkly, like a thundercloud that had fallen from the sky. I could smell a bonfire bitterness on the night air, and it made my heart thump. I told myself it wasn't a frightening smell at all; it smelt like autumn walks in Hyde Park – like Guy Fawkes Night, Hallowe'en . . .

If Robert were here, I told myself, *he wouldn't be afraid at all.*

I stared into the dark mass of trees ahead, and my imagination ambushed me with nightmarish creatures – slavering wolves, whispering tree-demons, long-fingered witches . . . Every part of me was alive with fear now – my fingers, my skin, my lungs . . .

And then a sudden, desperate shriek pierced the night like a needle.

I froze. *An owl?* But it sounded almost human . . .

I turned back to look at the house – and stifled a scream.

Tall shadows were moving in an upstairs window. A crowd of twisted silhouettes – three people – no, four! Who on earth could it be, upstairs in our house so late at night? Father, Mama, Nanny Jane and . . . *who else?*

Another cry escaped from the window, the shadows danced in a flurry of movement, and then there was a longer scream. A pitiful wail.

It wasn't an owl.

It was Mama.

3

I ran. I pelted back through the open kitchen door, through the kitchen and up the stairs – *Mama, my Mama* . . .

Halfway up the stairs, gasping for breath, I froze. There were voices – deep and earnest – then the door of Mama's room opened and Father walked out, followed by Nanny Jane. I caught a glimpse of a large, shadowy figure before the door was firmly closed again.

Nanny Jane looked deadly serious, but she smiled brightly as soon as she saw me. Suspiciously brightly.

'What's wrong? What's wrong with Mama?' I said, trying to control my panicked breathing.

Father opened his mouth to say something, then he closed it, shaking his head. He walked past me and down the stairs.

'What's wrong with her, Nanny Jane?' I repeated. 'Can I see her? Who's that in her room?'

'Today was a bit much for your mother, Henry,' Nanny Jane said. 'She's just rather confused and upset. But she's sleeping now. Your father called a doctor and he has given her some medicine.' She took a deep breath and tried to smile again. 'And now you need to get to bed too, young lady,' she continued, steering me into my bedroom. 'What are you doing up at this hour anyway? Why are you wearing your boots?'

I didn't have a chance to answer, or to ask her any more questions. I was tucked up tightly beneath the soft blue blanket before I knew what was happening. The clock in the hallway struck half past the hour. *Half past what?* I wondered.

When I was smaller and couldn't sleep, Mama would sit beside me on the bed and read to me by candlelight. But I wasn't small any more. And Mama was ill – so ill that Father had sent for a doctor in the middle of the night . . .

I picked up my book of fairy tales and turned to the Hans Christian Andersen story, *The Nightingale*. This was Mama's favourite. I read about the Emperor of China and how he had kept a nightingale in a cage to sing for him. One day the Emperor was given a present – a mechanical nightingale encrusted with precious jewels. He was so enchanted by his new toy that he released the real nightingale, who flew joyously back to the forest. But the toy nightingale soon broke and the Emperor became very ill.

The most beautiful illustration was at the end of the story – the Emperor's room in the royal palace. The square bed was swathed with red and gold cloth, golden lanterns hung from the ceiling, the jewelled nightingale sat silently inside a gilded cage. Death loomed over the Emperor, drawn as a skeleton in a Chinese robe. Behind the bed was a large open window which revealed the hills and forest beyond the palace walls. In the middle of the window, just about to fold her little brown wings and alight on the sill, was the nightingale. She had returned to the dying Emperor, to drive away Death with the beauty of her song.

I awoke in a knot of sheets and blankets in an unfamiliar bed. It took me a moment to remember that we had moved house. The events of the previous night floated, piece by piece, back into my head – my walk in the dark garden, Mama's unearthly shrieking, the shadowy doctor in her room . . . In the morning light these horrors felt like the echoes of a bad dream: even as my mind reached for them, they melted away. The curtains were open and soon the whole room was filled with green-gold summer light.

I decided to have porridge for breakfast. This felt like an important decision, as I hadn't been in the habit of eating much breakfast. I wanted moving house to be a fresh start, just like Father had said. I wanted to make my days feel solid and normal and real again, and porridge seemed to be a good way to begin.

In the kitchen, Nanny Jane filled my bowl almost up to the top and stirred it with thick, golden honey. I took it into the dining room.

Father sat at the table, reading a letter.

How thin and pale he looked. Since Robert had gone, bruised circles had appeared beneath his eyes. He looked like a man who had been put through a mangle or stretched on a rack, but, as always, he was immaculately shaven, smartly dressed, and his thick dark hair was neatly combed and parted. I felt an overwhelming surge of love for him.

'Good morning, Father,' I said.

He didn't reply, he just reached for the teapot and poured more tea without taking his eyes from the letter. The tea spilt and bloomed on the white table-cloth in front of him, and I handed him a napkin.

'Oh! Good morning, Henry,' he said.

'Good morning, Father,' I said again.

He looked back at his letter, raising his teacup to his lips. Scarred skin stretched, like a map of Africa, across the back of his hand and wrist. Many men bore scars these days – reminders of the Great War that had ended last November – but Father had not fought. He was an engineer and had spent most of the war working in the ports and factories of Britain; fighting for victory, yes, but not actually fighting. Father's scar was not from the war at all. I tried not to think about the night he got it.

'I like the new house,' I lied. 'And the garden. And my room is lovely.'

He nodded and pulled at his moustache.

'How is Mama today?'

Father said nothing for a moment, then he drew out his watch. 'The doctor will be calling again shortly to check on her.'

He turned back to the letter in his hand. It was trembling. After a while he said, 'It looks as if I – I may have to go abroad for a while, Henry. To work.'

'Go where?' I asked, my heart beating quickly. *But we have only just got here . . .*

Father didn't answer my question. 'I'm sorry,' he muttered, so quietly I almost thought I had imagined it. 'I'm sorry. I think – I really must go.' He wasn't looking at me, and I wasn't sure he was even aware he had spoken out loud. He folded the letter and tucked it in his jacket pocket. Then he stood and left the room, absently touching my shoulder as he passed me.

I heard him making a telephone call from the hallway, speaking loudly into the mouthpiece about tickets, trains and sailing times. Then he went upstairs to pack.

Something is terribly wrong, I thought. *With Father, or Mama. Or both of them.* I couldn't eat any porridge at all.

At nine o'clock I opened the front door to a tall, fat man dressed in a tweed suit and carrying a bulging black leather bag. He had a white moustache and bushy eyebrows. He might have looked like a friendly old giant, except for his bulging eyes, and a thick, purple lower lip that stuck out.

'You must be young Henrietta,' he said, putting out a huge hand. 'Your father told me all about you last night. I'm Doctor Hardy.'

I pressed my lips together and shook his hand firmly (I once heard Father telling Robert about the importance of a strong handshake). The doctor's hand was damp and flabby but its tight grip made me wince.

'Is Mama . . . ?' But I couldn't finish my question.

Doctor Hardy bent down and spoke to me as if I were five years old instead of twelve. His breath smelt of kippers and stale tea.

'Mummy isn't very well, Henrietta,' he said, still gripping my hand. 'She needs special medicine so she can get some rest.'

Nanny Jane appeared from the kitchen.

'Doctor Hardy,' she said crisply. 'Let me take you upstairs to see Mrs Abbott.'

Father left at lunchtime. When I kissed him goodbye he

put his arms around me, but it was as if I wasn't really there. He kissed Piglet and spoke quietly to Nanny Jane for a few moments, then he walked to the car.

He blames me, I thought, perhaps for the hundredth time. *He blames me for what happened in London. That's why he's leaving us.*

We were all smiling – flat little painted-on half-smiles – but my eyes burned and my throat hurt. I clamped my teeth tightly together and smiled a bit more to stop myself from crying. Only Piglet actually looked upset, although that was probably because she was hungry. She was always hungry.

The motor car paused at the bottom of the drive-way, next to the sign that said HOPE HOUSE. I waved as the car rolled out on to the road and disappeared from view. I waved because Nanny Jane was waving. She waved Piglet's hand for her too.

Mama hadn't come outside to say goodbye, but I looked up as we walked back into the house and saw a shadow at her bedroom window. Two white hands were pressed to the glass.

4

After Father left, I lost track of the days. Some-how, it felt as if every day was Sunday. I spent hours reading on a blanket in the garden, in the shade of a huge sycamore tree. I read the same books over and over again – *Alice's Adventures in Wonderland*, *The Secret Garden*, *The Wind in the Willows*, my fairy tales . . . These were the books of my childhood. They were familiar, safe. I knew how they ended.

The nights were long and lonely. My dreams grew darker and more terrifying: I was haunted by a terrible sobbing sound and sometimes sudden shrieks that left me shivering and sweating in terror. And the smell – always that choking smell of smoke.

Doctor Hardy came and went, dispensing his pills and his advice.

'Run along now,' he would say, reaching out to pluck a book from my hands. 'Little girls like you shouldn't be reading stories all day, Henrietta – you should be learning something useful, like needlework.' He would bend his grinning face down towards mine as he spoke, and I would be transfixed by the glistening threads of saliva strung between his teeth.

'Yes, Doctor Hardy,' I would say, and my voice would be flat. I felt flat inside too. Flat and empty, like a book with all the pages torn out.

I didn't see Mama often. She stayed in her room. She had not been well since last summer, but since our move here, and since Father had left, she seemed to be much, much worse. She looked exhausted – deeply exhausted, right through to her bones.

On the journey from London, Father had told me that he, Mama and Robert had come here on holiday before I was born. They had stayed in an old lighthouse keeper's cottage by the sea. Coming to live here at Hope House was supposed to make Mama better, but she wasn't getting better, she was getting worse. It was as if she was becoming a ghost.

Most mornings I played with Piglet, or pushed her pram around the garden. I enjoyed our slow, day-dreamy walks. I stuck to the paths and stayed away from the strange shadows of the wood.

I helped Nanny Jane with any jobs that needed doing, and I visited our new cook, Mrs Berry, in the kitchen. Sometimes I would help her beat eggs or whip cream. She was always pleased to see me and would give me iced lemonade and thick wedges of freshly baked bread smothered in butter and raspberry jam, whether I was hungry or not.

Mrs Berry talked a lot. She talked about all her family and neighbours as if I knew exactly who they were, and soon enough I felt as if I did. I didn't say much. I learnt to ask the sort of questions she enjoyed answering.

One afternoon I helped Mrs Berry make bread. I kneaded the dough until my hands ached. Mrs Berry let me shape the dough into little bread rolls. I made plaits and knots and flowers and animals.

'What's that one supposed to be?' Mrs Berry asked.

'A tortoise,' I said.

'It looks more like a squashed mouse.' Mrs Berry laughed, and I laughed too, brushing my hair away from my eyes and getting flour all over my face. That made us laugh even more. And then suddenly, without any warning, I was missing Robert desperately. Something burned in my throat. Tears welled up in my eyes and I backed away from the table.

'I'm just going outside for a breath of air, Mrs Berry,' I managed to say, heading for the back door. I needed to escape.

I had left the book I was reading — *Little Women* — on a rug in the garden earlier that morning. I had read it twice before, but it was a good book to read when I was feeling lonely. I wanted to read books about families. I would imagine I was just one of a crowd of squabbling, giggling siblings, and pretend I had a bossy big sister or a best friend there to take charge and sort everything out. Every now and then, when I was sure no one could hear me, I would find myself talking to this imaginary friend. Sometimes she was like Jo in *Little Women* – funny and tomboyish and practical. I would hear her voice in my mind – warm and reassuring. But on this hot, humid afternoon, my imaginary friend was different – more separate from me, more real. And it wasn't a girl, it was a boy . . .

Robert.

He lay on his back in the shade of the old gazebo, gazing up into the mess of honeysuckle above.

I stood perfectly still on the lawn and stared. It was as if I saw him through a mist at first – he was blurred, more like a drawing than a real boy, like an illustration from a storybook. His hair was lighter, and he seemed younger than when I had last seen him. I walked closer and knelt down beside him. I wanted to reach out and touch his hand . . . *But you're imagining him*, I said to myself. *You're just imagining him . . .*

'It's nice here, Hen,' Robert said. I saw that he had a runner bean in his hand and wondered if he had taken it from the kitchen garden. He gnawed at it. 'I might keep you company for a while. If that's all right.'

'Y-yes,' I said, faltering. I tried to smile. 'Yes.'

He leant back on his elbows, closed his eyes and tilted up his chin, as if he were drinking in the sunshine. The golden light shimmered on his hair.

'A lovely place,' he murmured. 'Hope House. A new chapter, Hen. Hope for us all here, don't you think?'

I didn't know what to say.

'Let's explore,' Robert said, sitting up and shading his eyes with a freckled hand. 'Do you want to go for a walk in the woods?'

I looked towards the wilderness at the bottom of the garden.

'I'll come with you if you like – if you're scared . . .'

I felt a flash of bravery. 'Yes,' I said. 'Let's.' But then I stopped. A cloud of rooks rose up from the branches of the tallest trees, cawing loudly. Something must have startled them . . . The leaves whispered darkly in the breeze. 'Maybe another day,' I said, trying not to sound frightened.

Robert just smiled before lying back in the long grass. 'The woods will still be there tomorrow, Hen,' he said.

I shook my head. *It can't be Robert*, I thought. *It can't be him* . . . I closed my eyes against the bright sunlight, and when I opened them again, he had vanished.

Nanny Jane was there, though. She was standing on the terrace, her arms folded in front of her. She had a strange expression on her face, and she was staring straight at me.

I stood up quickly, turned my back on her and walked towards the sycamore tree. I sat down on the rug and picked up my book, moving my eyes back and forth over the words, but they were just meaningless patterns on the page. I was breathing quickly now, in strange little gasps. I stared at the book, desperate to lose myself in the story in front of me so I wouldn't have to listen to my own thoughts. *It can't be Robert. It can't be . . .*

I couldn't help it. I looked back at the gazebo, hoping that my brother would have mysteriously reappeared. He wasn't there, but the sunlight danced on the dry grass – a flash of gold, just like his hair . . . I shook my head again, struggling to control the sobs that were welling up in my chest.

'Robert is dead,' I told myself. 'He's gone. He died last summer.'

5

D octor Hardy visited that evening.

'And how is our little cherub?' he enquired, bending low and breathing in my face. Today he reeked of cooking fat – smoky lard, the burnt bits in a roasting tray.

He wasn't calling *me* a cherub, he was referring to Piglet, who was freshly bathed and snuggled up on my shoulder, ready for bed. He reached out with a fat, purple finger and stroked her cheek.

'She's quite well, thank you,' I said, moving her to my other shoulder.

'And how about you, Miss Abbott?' He looked into my eyes, moving his head from side to side like a snake charmer. 'Slightly jaundiced, do you think, Miss Button?'

'I think she's just caught the sun a little, actually,' said Nanny Jane. 'She's been outside a lot.'

'Ah,' said the doctor. 'Not wandering too far, I hope. No big adventures for you, young lady – you need a nice, quiet summer holiday, don't you?'

'Of course,' Nanny Jane said quickly. 'She's been . . . doing needlework, haven't you, Henry?'

I nodded gratefully. Piglet started grumbling.

The doctor reached out quickly with his big hands and took her from me. It felt as if someone had just pulled a handful of guts from my abdomen. I nearly gasped with the shock. He held Piglet up to his face.

'What's wrong, baby?' he cooed, sickeningly. 'What's wrong? Oh, you're not happy at all, are you?'

Doctor Hardy wanted there to be something wrong with everyone. *Perhaps it makes him feel more important*, I thought, *if everyone is ill*.

Piglet's grumble turned into a full-throated cry.

'She's just very tired, Doctor,' I said in my most grown-up voice, taking Piglet back again. I pressed her to my chest so that I was able to breathe once more. 'Sorry, it's past her bedtime. Good night.' And I carried her up the stairs.

Piglet's wail faded to a whimper. I tucked her into her cot and kissed her goodnight. She grunted and fussed a bit, but she was tired. 'Ladybird, ladybird fly away home,' I started to sing, stroking her soft hair. 'Your house is—' But then I stopped myself.

'Sweet dreams, Piglet,' I said, rather emptily.

Her eyes closed and soon she was whistling softly through her turned-up nose, her tummy rising and falling steadily.

Doctor Hardy and Nanny Jane came upstairs just a few minutes later. I heard glass bottles and metal instruments clinking and bumping around in his bag. The two of them were talking in hushed, secretive tones. They went straight into Mama's room and closed the door behind them. Then I heard the key turn in the lock.

Click. Locked. No entry.

No callers, hawkers or daughters, please . . .

Doctor Hardy stayed until about ten o'clock. He did not speak to me before he left, and Nanny Jane, who had brought me a cup of cocoa when she came to say goodnight, had not told me anything either. It was midnight now, and I was still not asleep.

Why would no one tell me anything? Father had left us. Mama was so sick I hardly ever saw her. I wanted to help. I wanted to do *something*, but it was the middle of the night and I was all by myself and I was twelve years old. What could I possibly do?

I stared out of the window at the moonlit garden and the dark woodland beyond. There it was again — that mysterious wisp of smoke drifting up from the trees — that flicker of faery flame that I had seen on our first night at Hope House. There was someone out there in the darkness. *Someone or something.* I felt that familiar tugging sensation – a voice calling to me from among the trees . . .

Doctor Hardy's instruction echoed in my mind: *No big adventures for you, young lady . . .*

I smiled a small, angry smile.

I would go.

At the very bottom of the garden, where the wilderness began, I stopped and stared into the blackness. Then I took one long, deep breath and walked into the dark jaws of the forest.

In the woods, the moon and the stars generated something that couldn't quite be called light. They didn't shine, they silvered the darkness, creating just enough dusty grey shadow for me to pick my way through the trees. I kept one hand in front of my face so I didn't walk into any low branches, and twice I felt the sticky threads of spiders' webs breaking over my fingers. The smell of smoke grew stronger. A faint yellow haze glowed in the gloom and I followed it, stumbling along dark, twisting paths, until at last I saw the light of a fire flickering in a clearing ahead.

I hid behind an oak tree, pressing my palms and cheeks against the rough bark. I could hear nothing but the gentle crackling of burning wood. It didn't sound like the sort of fire that haunted my dreams; it sounded like a friendlier sort of fire – for toasting crumpets and warming your hands. This was no faery flame, this was real. Someone was here, sitting beside a fire in the woods of Hope House . . .

Slowly, very slowly, I peered around the tree. There was a round campfire exactly in the middle of the clearing . . . There was no one sitting beside it. At the far edge of the clearing, beyond the fire and several yards of leaf-strewn earth, stood a small gypsy caravan. It was old and battered and looked as if it were somehow part of the forest itself, growing out of the bramble bushes that surrounded it. It might once have been yellow, like Toad's caravan in *The Wind in the Willows*, but much of the paint had peeled off to reveal the bare, rotting wood beneath. Dirty lace curtains were drawn across two tiny, broken windows. At the foot of the wooden steps lay what looked like an old rowing boat, filled with soil and planted with herbs.

The plants suddenly bent and shivered strangely, as if touched by an invisible hand. Something was moving in the dark space beneath the caravan. Something twisting and squirming, as dark as the darkness itself. A pair of eyes blinked – they were looking straight into mine. A thump of fear hit me and I stood perfectly still. The eyes blinked again, and a lean, dark shape squeezed out from beneath the caravan. It was a cat – a bedraggled little brownish-black cat. It stalked towards the trees, black against the almost-blackness of the woods. As it moved further from the light of the fire, I could only see it because I already knew it was there.

A chunk of wood shifted in the campfire, showering sparks on to the leafy floor of the forest. I couldn't help myself – with a gasp of fear, I ran forward and stamped on the sparks until they were extinguished.

'*Who's that?*' a voice asked suddenly, just a few yards away.

I stumbled back behind my tree, my heart banging painfully.

Immediately, I heard the voice again, hissing from the caravan window: '*Is that you, cat?*'

The cat meowed an insolent reply and melted into the darkness. Then the door of the caravan flew open.

I held my breath, terrified, hypnotized.

A ghastly figure stepped into the clearing, the shadows of the moonlit trees creating a cage of darkness around it. It spread its scraggy arms wide and a ragged blanket opened like reptilian wings. It stared into the darkness, searching, hunting . . . Its face was lit by the fire now – a woman's face, white as bone – feral, hollow and dangerous. Her hair was a mess of thick, twisted snakes. I thought of the Sea Witch in *The Little Mermaid*. I thought of Medusa . . . Her stony stare penetrated the darkness and found me there, clinging to my tree. She breathed in – a slow, crackling gasp. I didn't hide. I just stood there, petrified. Her head jerked down and her elbows shot up in two bony points so that she looked like a spider about to leap upon its prey. I opened my mouth to scream, but I couldn't make a sound. Her eyes burned into me. She took another step forward, curled back her lips, and hissed . . .

And I ran.

6

I could hardly speak at breakfast the next morning. Every time I moved my head I saw a scrawny black cat crawling in the shadows under the furniture. Every time I blinked I saw the witch's face seared on the insides of my eyelids – a terrible face, white with anger, frozen in a vicious hiss . . . I couldn't eat anything. Nanny Jane kept frowning at me.

There was a knock at the front door and a few seconds later Mrs Berry came into the dining room. She passed a telegram to Nanny Jane, and the eyes of the two women met meaningfully. I knew it was a look I was not supposed to have seen. Nanny Jane opened the telegram and glanced at it quickly before refolding it and placing it beneath a pile of other letters.

I stared at her. *Well?*

She said nothing. She poured herself a cup of tea.

Eventually I said, 'Was that a telegram, Nanny Jane?'

She looked at me as if to say, *You know perfectly well it was a telegram, young lady.* Then she said, 'It's from your father. His work has taken him to Italy and he doesn't think he'll be able to come home for a while yet.'

I took a moment to consider this. 'To *Italy*?'

'Until November.'

'Until *November*?'

'Please try to stop being a Polly parrot, Henry.'

'But November is *months* away. He can't stay away from us that long.'

'He's working, Henry. He has to work . . .'

'What else did he say?'

Nanny Jane's lips pursed and tightened. *That's enough questions.* She didn't say it out loud, but she didn't need to. What wasn't she telling me?

Half an hour later, Nanny Jane announced that she needed to go to the nearby village, Little Birdham, to send a telegram to Father in reply. I waved as she wheeled Piglet's perambulator down the driveway. And while I waved, I made a plan . . .

As soon as they had gone, I closed the front door and ran up the stairs. I paused for a moment: my bedroom was in front of me; to my right was the darker section of landing leading to my parents' rooms and bathroom; the corridor to my left led to the nursery and Nanny Jane's room. I turned left and walked straight to her room, trying to ignore the warnings of my conscience as I twisted the door knob.

The door opened to reveal a small, bright bedroom that smelt of lavender and starched linen. I had never seen inside Nanny Jane's room before, but it was pleasingly familiar. The bed was neatly made with white sheets and a floral counterpane; a Jane Austen novel — *Pride and Prejudice* — sat on the pillow. A white-painted door opened on to the adjoining nursery.

I was all prepared to play Sherlock Holmes, but I didn't need to search very hard: on the dressing table, next to a hairbrush and Nanny Jane's coin purse, lay the pile of letters, and there at the bottom was Father's telegram.

My hands shook as I unfolded the paper and read the typed message.

```
Not home for several months Italy and
then Switzerland until November STOP
Do not give permission for Mrs A
admittance STOP Tell Dr H treatment
must be given at home for now STOP
Will write STOP
```

I read it several times, trying to make sense of the oddly abrupt words. His work was going to keep him abroad until at least November. He didn't give

permission for Mama's admittance. *Admittance to what?*
I remembered Nanny Jane's tightened lips and her
whispered conversations with Doctor Hardy.

I took care to leave everything exactly as I had found
it and closed the door behind me. I felt a wave of relief
– and then guilt. It wasn't nice to go snooping in other
people's rooms.

The corridor stretched darkly ahead of me, ending
with the sealed silence of Mama's room. I felt another
surge of guilt as I turned the handle of her door. It was
locked.

Locked from the inside or the outside? Was she a prisoner, or did she simply want to be left alone?

I imagined her in there, staring up at the cracked
ceiling . . .

I knocked softly.

There was only silence. I pressed my ear to the thick
wood but could hear nothing beyond the thudding of
my own pulse.

'Mama?' I called.

No reply.

I knelt down and looked through the keyhole.
Nanny Jane would go berserk if she knew what I was
up to – sneaking into other people's rooms, spying
through keyholes – *Hardly appropriate behaviour for a
young lady, Henrietta!* It was too dark to see much
through the keyhole – just a vague shape in the bed.

'Mama?' I called again, my voice buzzing against the

wood, so close to my lips.

The shape in the bed moved and I thought I heard a sound like a low sob. Then there was silence once more.

I sat there for some time, my back against the door, trying to decide what to do. I had read about people opening locks with hairpins, but that was just in stories . . . Then I remembered the locking of Mama's door the previous night. *Doctor Hardy*, I thought. *Doctor Hardy has done this.* Anger surged through me. I wished I could grow into a giant, like Alice. People would have to listen to me if I were nine feet tall: *You're nothing but a pack of cards . . .*

As my thoughts drifted, I noticed an odd thing about the wooden panelling beside Mama's door. The dark wood was patterned with carved lines and squares, but here, at the edge of one pattern, were two hinges.

It was a small door.

A cupboard? I followed the line of the door up, right and down, and found a keyhole. It was so small and so carefully placed that it looked like a knot in the wood. There was no door knob or handle. I tried to prise the door open with my fingers but the crack around the edge was much too narrow. My fingernails filled with scrapings of old sticky varnish and dirt. I pressed against the door in frustration and, to my surprise, it clicked and sprang open.

7

I t wasn't a cupboard.

Beyond the little door rose a steep, narrow flight of carpeted stairs. I stooped below the opening, taking care to pull the door almost shut behind me.

The stairs were thick with dust and smelt of mould and mouse droppings. I sneezed twice and then started to climb, slowly and carefully. Sunlight shone through the dusty air above me as through a morning mist. I had the strange thought that I might somehow appear in a story-book world above the clouds, or in the turret of a fairy-tale castle.

At the top of the staircase, I found myself in the middle of a square attic. I stood quite still. I remembered the smells of our attic in London – the attic

Robert and I used to play in – sawdust and books and rusty Meccano; enamel paint and glue for all Robert's model trains and ships . . . Panicked memories flapped around me like bats. I beat them back – *No, that was a different attic, Hen, a different house* . . . I looked around. Ancient wooden beams sloped up to an apex above the staircase and directly in front of me was a large round window, as big as a cartwheel. It overlooked the driveway at the front of the house, and the patchwork of fields and woodland beyond stretched all the way to the sparkling blue sea.

I could see a white lighthouse standing on a distant cliff, and wondered if it was the one Mama, Father and Robert had visited before I was born. I touched the windowpane with my fingertips. The glass was gritty with dust.

Dust clung to the rotten window frame, too, to a wooden toy chest at the foot of a narrow bed, and to everything else in the room. On a shelf on the wall a row of model ships sat becalmed in dust, their rigging thick with cobwebs, like a fleet of miniature *Mary Celestes*. I felt a swift, sharp pain of recognition in my chest. This was a boy's bedroom, or it *had* been, once. A boy like Robert, perhaps. A row of books on a low shelf by the window included *Treasure Island*, *Peter and Wendy*, *South Sea Tales*, *Moonfleet* . . .

I picked up the copy of *Moonfleet* and held it gently in my palm. Then I allowed the pages to fall open as they wished. It was a favourite game of mine with other people's books. The thick, yellowed pages parted and fell quite naturally near the end, and I read the description of 'Maskew's Match' – the lamp lit nightly by Grace Maskew to guide her long-lost love, John Trenchard, safely back home.

I closed the book and looked once more around the room. Cobwebs hung in great swathes from the rafters. One long, dusty tendril dangled almost to the floor. My eyes fell upon the wooden toy chest and, my head filled with those tales of peril and adventure, I immediately thought of smugglers' gold and pirate treasure.

Very carefully, I opened the lid, expecting to be blinded by a gleam of diamonds and doubloons . . .

But it was full of toys. A broken kite, tangled in its own strings; a ship's telescope; a wooden sword, the handle worn quite smooth. I felt a pang of conscience. For the second time that morning, I was aware that I was trespassing. No one had told me not to go into this room – no one had told me it even existed – but I felt a sick, guilty feeling in my stomach, as if I had accidentally trodden on someone's grave. I closed the lid of the toy box gently and wiped my hands on my pinafore.

From far below, echoing through the hallway, up the stairs and through the secret doorway, I heard the metallic pounding of the knocker on the front door. My heart pounded back, as if in reply. I froze. The cobweb dangling above me swung in an invisible breeze. I crept back down the dusty stairs.

The little wooden door clicked shut behind me and I tiptoed down the landing. When I heard Nanny Jane's voice in the hallway, I froze once more. *How had she returned from the village so quickly?* For a moment I entertained the thought that the attic room was indeed part of a fairy-tale world and that my five minutes there had, perhaps, been five hours in the real world . . .

'I'm absolutely sure,' Nanny Jane was saying in what I recognized as her coolest, firmest voice. 'This is the Abbott family. They've been renting Hope House since the beginning of the summer.'

I heard the lower tones of a man's voice, though I couldn't make out what he was saying.

'No,' Nanny Jane replied. 'I'm sorry – I can't answer your questions just now. Mrs Berry might be able to help you, though. Could you call at a more convenient time, perhaps? . . . Very well. Goodbye.' She closed the door, and I didn't have to see her face to know her lips were tightly pursed.

'Who was that?' I asked, clumping innocently down the stairs.

'A rather strange man,' she said, shaking her head.

'How are you back from the village so soon, Nanny Jane?' I added.

'Questions, questions, questions,' she said impatiently as she passed me on the stairs. 'I forgot my purse.' As she marched towards her bedroom, I thanked my lucky stars I hadn't been caught in there, snooping.

I crossed the hallway, passed Piglet's parked pram, and opened the front door very quietly. We had had very few visitors since moving to Hope House and I was curious.

The thin, dark figure of a man was walking down the drive, away from the house. I had never seen him before. His swift, uneven gait, and a walking stick shooting out to his side, made him look like a scuttling spider.

8

'This one's sure to tempt your mother, Miss Henrietta,' Mrs Berry said.

It was a few days later and we were in the kitchen, making a cake. I stirred lemon juice and orange peel into the batter, breathing in the fresh, bright sweetness. I didn't say anything, but I didn't think it was likely that Mama could be cured by a St Clement's cake. Through the open window I heard a bird squawking noisily; something must have frightened it. I looked out into the garden just in time to see a small dark cat slinking into the hedge and vanishing. I blinked. *Was it the cat from the forest? The witch's cat?*

Mrs Berry tried again: 'Saw you out in the garden this morning, Miss,' she said, breaking two eggs into a bowl, 'taking your little sister out for a bit of sunshine as usual. Our country air will do you both the power of good after all that London smog. Little Miss Roberta's ever such a bonny girl, isn't she? No danger of *her* losing her appetite!'

I agreed, concentrating on mixing the batter, trying to get every last bit of flour off the edges of the bowl. My eyes were heavy from another sleepless night. The mysterious limping man who had appeared at our door a few days ago had somehow crept inside my head. He scuttled through my nightmares like an insect.

Mrs Berry inclined her head towards me and whispered dramatically, 'Now, you must be careful on those walks of yours, Miss Henrietta. Just you stay in the garden – there's all sorts of terrors in the deep, dark woods, you know!' She was smiling but her eyes were wide with mock-horror.

I tried to look suitably mock-scared. Inside, I was genuinely frightened. The very idea of heading back into those dark woods was enough to make me feel ill: I felt a painful pulsing behind my eyes. I kept stirring the cake mixture.

'What do you mean?' I asked.

'Well, folks round here say there's a witch living in Nightingale Wood . . . A real witch with a broomstick and everything. She'll turn you into a toad, soon as look at you!'

'Goodness!' I said. Fear crackled in my chest.

'My little nephew was in those woods in the autumn, looking for conkers, and he said the witch shrieked curses at him and chased him on her broomstick like a hellish harpy.' She chuckled. 'Poor little chap won't go in there at all now!'

I didn't know what to say, so I said, 'Goodness!' again and laughed. I swallowed hard.

While Mrs Berry talked, my mind was dragged helplessly back to that night in the woods. I saw the witch, lit by the flickering fire – her bone-white face, her snake-hair, her wild, staring eyes . . .

'Give it here, Miss,' Mrs Berry said gently, taking the bowl and the wooden spoon from me and beating the cake mixture until it looked like satin. She poured the batter into a round metal tin, scraping the bowl noisily, then passed the wooden spoon back to me and winked; it was covered in thick, sweet cake mixture.

I walked down to the bottom of the garden, right to the fringes of the forest – as close as I dared to go. There was a pond here, tucked away in a shady corner. Beside the pond stood a mossy wooden bench with a high back and sides – perfect for a smallish girl to curl up on. I spread a blanket on the bench and sat there for a while, a copy of *The Railway Children* on my lap, watching the goldfish drifting about, and trying to spot the improbable little faces of the frogs poking out of the water. My head was still aching and I felt a bit dizzy. There was a peculiar kind of heat and pressure behind my eyes. I took a few lungfuls of Mrs Berry's good country air, and opened my book.

Father and Mama had given me *The Railway Children* for my tenth birthday. Father had chosen it because of its title – he was a railway engineer. That was what he was doing in Italy right now: designing new tracks, bridges and tunnels.

In London, Father used to come home from work with bundles of plans – drawings and calculations which Robert and I loved to look at. I thought they were beautiful – a precise tangle of straight lines and tiny, pencilled symbols, but the numbers meant nothing to me; I couldn't connect them to anything solid. For Robert, it was as if the numbers just sprang into the air and became something real . . .

I wondered if my imagination would be able to conjure him up again. I closed my eyes and pictured him in the London attic, playing with his model trains. 'More coal for the engine!' he would shout, moving the train more quickly along the track. 'More coal, fire-boy!'

Fire-boy . . . I opened my eyes and looked up into the white sky above. A beautiful image appeared – a boy born of fire, like a human phoenix. I saw a child created by flames – a laughing, burning boy-god. Flaming wings rose from his back and he became an angel, glorious with light.

I closed my eyes tightly again until the image dissolved. Then I tried to concentrate on my book.

I had been reading for about twenty minutes when an odd feeling crept over me. I was certain I was not alone.

Robert?

No . . .

I looked up from the pages of my book and saw a small brown and black cat sitting neatly on the far side of the pond. It was the witch's cat. It was staring into the water, following the movement of a fat goldfish with its yellow-green eyes.

'Hello,' I whispered.

The cat looked up at me, and then looked back at the goldfish. It leant forward, shifting its weight so it could raise a front paw. It reached out and touched the water, springing back again when the cold water rippled and the fish darted away.

Then it looked straight at me and blinked very slowly. It walked around the pond, right up to my legs, and rubbed its cheek on my knee. For a second, I thought it was going to hiss or bite me, but it didn't. Instead, it made a throaty little squeak, turned away, and disappeared into the gloom of the forest, just like Alice's white rabbit vanishing down the rabbit hole.

I stood up, and sat down again.

'*Go on, Hen,*' Robert's voice seemed to whisper. '*Go on . . . Or are you scared?*'

I stood up.

And followed it.

9

As I walked, Mrs Berry's words of broomsticks and harpies twisted into visions of terror in my mind. . . *Was there really a witch in the woods?*

I told myself I was too old to believe in such things, but as soon as I left the garden behind and entered the strange silence of the forest I started shivering. I kept walking, though. I needed to see her. I needed to see if I could be brave. My head was pounding now and my throat was swollen and sore.

The cat trotted ahead of me, its dark fur camouflaged against the forest floor. Every now and then – when I felt most afraid – I thought I caught a glimpse of Robert darting amongst the trees, his honey-gold hair shimmering in the dappled sunlight. I felt better knowing he was close by.

There were many paths through the undergrowth – made by forest creatures, I thought – and, although I had been this way before, I couldn't have described the route or drawn it on a map. It was as if I was being pulled through the maze of trees by a kind of gravity. Even when I thought about turning back, my feet kept moving forward, following the cat. I thought of *The Pied Piper of Hamelin*, I thought of *The Red Shoes*. In stories, bad things happened to people who couldn't control their own feet.

Before long the trees started thinning and we came upon the clearing. The breeze blew a cloud of smoke towards me and I stopped, my hand flying up to cover my mouth. I felt my lungs cramping, trying to cough. *It's just woodsmoke, Hen*, I told myself, my eyes watering. *A campfire, a friendly fire*... The cat strutted straight into the clearing and trilled a greeting.

I hid behind a tree, unsure of what to do. I could hear someone moving around, muttering to the cat. Suddenly I felt very, very stupid. The last time I was here it had been quite clear that I had not been welcome; what exactly was I proposing to say to the witch – 'The cat invited me'?

The muttering stopped and then, from out of the thick silence, a voice said, 'I know you're there.'

I don't really know what happened next. I remember suddenly feeling very hot and not being able to catch my breath. I remember the forest becoming a green ocean that swirled sickeningly before me. I remember the back of my head hitting the forest floor, dark stars bursting in my eyes and – for a moment – the treetops turning like carousel horses around a circle of blue sky above. Then there was nothing but darkness.

I awoke to the crackling of the campfire and the smell of cooking. I was lying on a blanket beside the fire and there beside me – so close I could almost have touched her – was the witch. She was singing some sort of chant or lullaby, so softly that I couldn't make out the words.

'You fainted,' she croaked.

She wasn't looking at me and I had barely moved. How did she know I was awake?

She spoke again. 'You're not well.' Her voice was rough and smooth at the same time, like sandpaper on old wood. It had a strange lilt to it – an accent I couldn't place.

I could feel the heat of the fire on my face, but I couldn't stop shivering. The witch got up, found another blanket and placed it over me.

'Thank you,' I managed to say.

She didn't reply; she sat back down and continued to gaze into the fire. She started singing her lullaby again. This time I could just make out the softly crooned words over the crackling of the flames:

Asleep ... O sleep a little while, white pearl ...

The cat was sitting between us, its paws neatly folded. It too stared at the fire. Then it rolled on to its side, stretched, and closed its eyes.

My vision was not quite sharp, and there was still that strange feeling of pressure inside my head. I wasn't entirely sure I was awake. The whole scene felt oddly familiar – as if I had dreamt it years before. And I wasn't as frightened as I should have been. Despite everything Mrs Berry had said, I felt strangely safe sitting here next to the witch – deep in the middle of the forest, as night approached . . . Perhaps it was the fact that she had wrapped a blanket around me. Perhaps it was the peacefully dozing cat at my side . . .

'You need looking after,' the witch said. 'A warm bed, hot food.'

I looked at her and, when my eyes eventually focused, I saw that she was much younger than I had first thought. Her hair was wild and her nails were dirty – but she wasn't an old woman at all. She couldn't have been much older than Mama, in fact. And she was strangely beautiful. Her skin was ghostly pale. Her eyes shone brightly in the firelight. She looked more like a forgotten, fairy-tale princess than a wicked witch.

'That was you the other night,' she said.

'Yes.'

'I thought it was the boys from the village, come to bother me again.' She smiled a crooked smile. 'I scare them off.' And she suddenly raised her arms so they became twisted, prehistoric wings again. My heart pounded at the sudden reappearance of this nightmare.

'I'm sorry I disturbed you,' I managed to say.

But the witch's eyes had returned to the fire. 'Go home now,' she said. 'Go back to Hope House . . .'

IO

I expected Nanny Jane to be waiting for me, but she was nowhere to be found. The gaslights glowed in the dining room and supper was on the table — two plates of lamb chops, vegetables and congealed gravy. One for me and one for Nanny Jane, but where was she? I took the glass of milk that had been set out for me and went to look upstairs. The unmistakable voice of Doctor Hardy drifted down from the landing, sticky and smug.

'Yes, it's worrying, certainly,' he said. 'And a fascinating case. My colleague — the doctor I mentioned to you previously — is particularly interested in female neurosis. He is currently making a study of chronic—'

And then they saw me.

'Oh, Henry,' said Nanny Jane, walking purposefully

towards me. 'I've told you before about losing track of the time like this. You've been out there for hours and hours—' She broke off and looked at me closely. 'Are you all right, Henry?'

'I – I think so,' I said. Why was she looking at me like that?

She put a hand flat on my forehead for a moment and then felt the heat of my cheeks with the backs of her fingers. She frowned at Doctor Hardy.

'Let's have a look at you, young lady,' he said, and I was shepherded into my room. Nanny Jane unlaced my boots as I sat on the bed. Doctor Hardy took my temperature and listened to my heart. I wondered if it was behaving normally; it seemed to do nothing but pound and panic these days. I squirmed underneath the doctor's cold stethoscope. I hated him being so close to me.

'A summer cold, probably,' he said (to Nanny Jane, not to me). 'She has a slight fever. Keep her in bed for now. Don't want her getting ill too, do we?'

'Of course,' Nanny Jane said, wetting a cloth with cool water from the jug at my wash-stand and pressing it to my forehead.

Then the doctor spoke more quietly to her, as if I wouldn't hear him if he lowered his voice. 'The fever might be psychosomatic, of course – if she's worrying too much about Mummy . . .'

Nanny Jane frowned again.

'I'll prescribe some Soothing Syrup – the morphine sulphate is excellent for treating anxiety in children.'

'Morphine sulphate?' Nanny Jane started. 'But—'

The doctor ignored her. 'Best to keep her away from Mrs Abbott for the time being,' he said. 'For both their sakes . . .'

Nanny Jane saw my frightened face, politely ushered the doctor from the room and took him downstairs. I finished my milk, used the damp wash-cloth to wipe my face, neck and hands, and then crept to the top of the staircase.

'About a week, I should think,' Doctor Hardy was saying. 'They should be ready for her then. I'll write to my colleague – he's really very keen to make Mrs Abbott part of his study. And I'll write to Mr Abbott again. As next of kin, he'll need to give his permission for the whole thing.'

For what whole thing? What study? Ready for what in about a week?

'I see,' Nanny Jane said. 'And what about the pills?'

'Morning, lunchtime and evening,' he replied, passing her a brown bottle from his bag. 'Mrs Abbott must be kept sedated for now . . .' He trailed off and there was a pause.

'I wish there was more we could do,' Nanny Jane said, quietly.

'We'll persist with the rest cure,' the doctor replied. 'Absolute peace and quiet. I will come over in a day or two to check on her. Please watch her closely. And when you're not with her, you must keep her door locked, Miss Button. Keep. It. Locked. It's for her own good. And do keep Henrietta and the baby away from her. Good night. '

The front door slammed.

I went back to my bedroom, wrapped the curtains around me and stared out of the black window.

There we were — Mama, Nanny Jane, Piglet and I — all under the same roof, but as separate and distant as four stars in the night sky. Each of us burning alone in the darkness.

II

Keep her door locked. Keep. It. Locked . . . Doctor
Hardy's command was cold and clanging –
like a key bouncing down the stone walls of a
well. It rang in my ears all night and into the following
morning.

I wanted to go and sit with Mama. I remembered
long evenings in London, cuddled up in my bed as she
read to me – the smell of her face cream and the
warmth of her arms around me. I wanted to feel her
arms around me now, but she was locked in her room
and I was not allowed to leave my bed.

Through the bedroom wall I could hear Nanny Jane
singing to Piglet as she put her down for her morning
nap – something about frogs jumping into ponds; it
sounded far too jolly to be a lullaby, but it was just

Piglet's sort of thing. When I heard Nanny Jane's footsteps on the landing, I called to her. She put her head around the door.

'Yes? Do you need anything?'

'Can I see Mama tomorrow, Nanny Jane?' I said. 'If I'm better?'

Nanny Jane sighed. 'Your mother really isn't well enough for visitors at the moment.'

'Not visitors – just me. I know she's ill, but I – maybe I could help . . .'

Nanny Jane shook her head.

'I just want to talk to her, Nanny Jane.'

'I'm sorry, Henry. She isn't – I don't think she has the strength for a conversation.'

My chest was aching now, as if something was swelling up inside me. I felt as if my ribs might crack with the pressure. There had to be something I could do, something I could say.

'I could just sit with her, perhaps. I promise I won't tire her out. I'll just hold her hand and sit with her.' Tears were rising up in my eyes. I swallowed hard and blinked them back. 'Maybe later in the week?'

'We'll see.' Nanny Jane came into the room and rearranged the blanket on my bed. Then she gave me a spoonful of Doctor Hardy's Soothing Syrup. It tasted disgusting. 'The doctor has given strict orders,' she said, 'and he knows best.' She looked at me, and something seemed to soften a little. 'I'm not saying no,

Henry. Perhaps next week. If she's a bit stronger.' Then she headed for the door.

'Back to sleep now, please,' she called over her shoulder.

But I didn't want to sleep. I opened my book of fairy tales and gazed at the picture of Rapunzel, locked in a lonely tower in the middle of the forest. The trees were much taller than the tower, so no sunlight could reach her window. I found myself sinking into the picture . . . And then I was there, standing in the forest below the tower, looking up at poor Rapunzel. But she wasn't Rapunzel any more, she was Mama. I called and called to her, but no sound came out of my mouth. Mama pounded with both fists on the door of her cell and the sound boomed through the forest like a giant heart-beat. I watched helplessly as she took a pair of huge scissors and cut off her own hair in thick, jagged hand-fuls until there was nothing left . . .

My pillow was wet with tears. I sat up, on the verge of screaming. I gasped and steadied my breath. The curtains were open, and a ray of late afternoon sunlight made a golden blur on the wallpaper. How long had I been asleep for? The sunbeam shimmered and danced, and then it became Robert. He sat down on a chair by the window and swung his legs back and forth.

'Robert,' I said gratefully, throwing off the blanket.

'Hello, Hen.' He smiled. He opened the window and leant his arms on the sill.

I could smell woodsmoke on the warm air that drifted through the window, and I thought about the witch beside her fire, stirring a cauldron of bubbling stew. I wondered if I would be brave enough to visit her again. I wanted to thank her for looking after me, but – I stopped myself – maybe it had all just been a strange dream . . .

'I want to go back into the woods,' I said. 'I need to see the witch again.'

'Let's go tonight,' he said, and his eyes gleamed at the thought of the adventure. 'You don't really think she's a witch, though, do you, Hen?'

'I think she's a good witch,' I said. 'She's very beautiful, Robert. Weirdly beautiful – like a ragged, long-ago princess, lost in the woods. Maybe she was cursed or enchanted somehow . . .'

Suddenly I realized that my bedroom door was open and someone was standing just outside it, staring at me through the dark gap. It was Nanny Jane.

'Who are you talking to, Henry?' she said sharply. 'I thought I heard you say—'

'No one,' I said. 'I'm not talking to anyone. I'm talking to myself.'

'Well, don't,' she snapped.

I glanced back towards the window where Robert sat, as still as a figure in a painting. Nanny Jane scanned the room. Her gaze slid straight over him.

'I was going to bring your sister in to see you,' she

said, still frowning, 'Would you like that, Henry?'

'Yes,' I said. 'Yes, please.'

Nanny Jane went to the nursery and came back with Piglet in her arms. My sister beamed at me and reached out with her fat little hands.

'Please could I take her outside and push her around the garden for a while?' I begged. 'I'm sure the fresh air would do me good . . .'

Nanny Jane shifted Piglet on to her hip, felt my forehead, asked me to stick out my tongue and then looked closely into my eyes. (I had no idea what she was looking for. Deceit, probably – she was eerily good at spotting that.) She hesitated, then made up her mind.

'No, Henry,' she said firmly. 'I'm sorry. Doctor Hardy said you were to rest today. I'll leave the baby with you, though – just for a few minutes' company.' She left the room still frowning, leaving the door ajar.

I stood at the window next to Robert, with Piglet nestled against my chest. The evening air was fragrant with flowers.

'What's that lovely smell?' I whispered. 'Stocks? Phlox? Mama would know . . .'

Robert gazed out of the window. 'Mama would know the Latin name too,' he said.

'Yes,' I said quietly.

Mama had studied Classics and she would sometimes help us with our Latin prep in the holidays.

'Have you learnt your vocab?' she would ask, and Robert would answer, '*A pedibus usque ad caput!*' – *From feet to head!*

I remembered Robert writing jokes and silly poems in Latin just to make Mama laugh. It was like their own secret language . . . I couldn't stick all that dry old grammar, or my dry old Latin schoolteacher either for that matter.

Piglet grumbled and wriggled in my arms. 'Shhh,' I said, stroking her hair.

Piglet's tufty hair promised to be like Robert's – soft and honey-coloured, rather than my thick, mousy tangle. And she had Robert's eyes too, with Mama's long, dark lashes.

'What will she be like when she gets bigger?' I wondered out loud. 'Will she be like me, do you think? Like Mama, or Father? Or like you?'

Robert studied Piglet. 'It's too early to tell,' he said, as if he were an expert in these matters.

I watched him looking at her and my throat hurt as I swallowed hard. The real Robert had never met his baby sister. Piglet had arrived just hours after Robert's funeral. I remembered Mama's hands tightening around her belly as the pains started, as if she wanted to keep the baby in. I think she knew then that she couldn't take care of her, that she was better off safe in the darkness inside her. I had heard the nurse whisper to Nanny Jane that Mama barely made a sound when the baby came. I wondered if Mama ever thought of Piglet, or if she even knew that she existed.

'I think she's a strong little thing,' Robert said at last.

He was right. Piglet was ready to fight for her own corner in life. In a strange sort of way I envied her. She was her own little being: clean and new and blissfully unaware of all the sadness she had been born into.

'Will she love stories like me, or maths, like you?'

'Perhaps both,' Robert countered with a smile.

I considered the possibility. Lewis Carroll had been both a writer and a mathematician. Perhaps it didn't have to be a battle between words and numbers, as it had so often been with Robert and me.

'Were we really so different, Hen?' Robert asked.

'Perhaps not,' I said, after a moment. 'But we weren't always very nice to each other, were we?'

I thought about that terrible argument we had had – the shouting, the name-calling, being sent to bed without supper . . .

'All brothers and sisters argue,' Robert said.

'But I said such horrid things.' *And that was the night you died . . .*

Robert sighed softly and looked out of the window again. An evening breeze shivered through the room, carrying my last words away from me, out of the window, and down the long garden, towards Nightingale Wood.

'Stories don't always have happy endings, Hen,' he said quietly.

12

I waited until Nanny Jane had gone to bed, then I crept from my room, closing my door as softly as I could, and tiptoed down the dark stairs.

Mrs Berry had baked a pie before going home for the evening and it was cooling on the kitchen table. I cut a warm, fat wedge and wrapped it in paper. It was polite to take a gift when you went calling.

I walked through the garden, past the rose bushes. I thought dizzily of the white roses in Wonderland, and the gardeners frantically painting them red for fear the Queen of Hearts would chop off their heads. I knew it was supposed to be funny, but I always felt too anxious for the poor gardeners to enjoy the silliness.

These roses smelt gorgeous, though – like honey and oranges. I thought how lovely it would be to take

Mama a rose from the garden . . . *If Nanny Jane won't let me see Mama*, I thought, *I'll just have to find a different way. Maybe the witch will help me . . .*

My feet took me where I wanted to go, twisting through the dark trees as if following a trail of moonlit stones or breadcrumbs only they could see. I came at last to the witch's clearing.

She was sitting beside her fire, wrapped in a cloak of old blankets. My memories of her song and her pale, beautiful face were all steeped in the strangeness of a dream, but she was here in front of me now and she seemed perfectly real.

She didn't take her eyes from the campfire. It was as if the fire itself burned in her eyes – the reflected flames danced dangerously. '*Shhh*,' she said, as I took a step towards her. I froze. Suddenly she swung around and fixed me with a terrible stare. She pointed her finger, as if she were about to put a curse upon me. I held my breath. But then the finger curled, and beckoned me. I sat down obediently on a pile of blankets near her. Near, but not too close.

Her cat was there. It rubbed its face on my knee and then sat between us. It sniffed at the wrapped slice of pie I had placed on the ground, and licked its nose. 'Listen,' the witch hissed, and my heart thudded. She pursed her lips and whistled a long, low whistle. '*Listen*,' she whispered again.

At first I heard nothing at all. I listened harder than

I had ever listened before. I started to hear the impossible sounds of trees growing, leaves rotting and worms tunnelling through the soil. Then quite suddenly, and all in a rush, birdsong poured through the warm summer air. It was a beautiful sound – liquid and sweet.

'What is it?' I breathed.

'A nightingale,' the witch whispered. 'This wood belongs to him, you know. Nightingale Wood.' And I thought I saw her eyes smile – just a little.

I thought of the nightingale in the Hans Christian Andersen story – the faithful little bird that returns to sing to the dying Emperor . . .

'A miraculous creature,' said the witch softly. 'Nothing much to look at – just a modest little brown bird, and yet there is nothing more beautiful than the nightingale's song.'

'I've never seen one,' I said, 'or even heard one before, but there's a lovely fairy tale about a nightingale . . .'

The witch nodded. I lay back in the blankets, gazing up at the perfect circle of starlit sky above.

'I wish Mama were here,' I whispered. 'I wish she could hear this too . . .' I thought of her alone in her room. 'But her door is locked. She couldn't get out even if she wanted to.'

'Locked?' the witch repeated.

'I'm not allowed to see her at all now . . .'

'Who says so?'

'Doctor Hardy.'

The witch's face seemed to twitch, and she muttered something under her breath. Then she said, 'Nobody has the right to do that. Especially not an old quack like Hardy . . .'

'You know him?'

Her face twitched again. 'If you need to see your mother,' she said, 'you must find a way of seeing her. I'm sure she needs to see *you* just as much.'

There was another burst of song from the nightin-gale, and the woods seemed to fill with a beautiful silver light. It was as if the stars had fallen into the forest, or the forest had risen up into the stars. I curled into the swan's nest of blankets and felt the fear and sadness in my heart melt away.

'You must find a way to see her,' the witch whis-pered thoughtfully. 'Old houses like that one, there's bound to be a spare key to her room somewhere . . .'

At this, I felt a tiny spark of hope and determination in my heart.

'Who are you?' I said.

'No one,' the witch replied. 'I'm not anyone. Not any more.'

'But – you must be *some*one . . .' Then a terrible thought struck me. 'Unless – unless I'm imagining you . . .'

The witch looked at me for a moment, and something in her face seemed to soften. Then she reached into a pocket concealed beneath one of her blankets and pulled out a tiny book – it looked like a bible. She took a piece of paper from between its pages and leant towards me.

'You're not imagining me,' she said.

I saw that it was not a piece of paper at all, but an old, torn photograph – a picture of a young woman in a smart nurse's uniform. Instead of smiling directly at the camera, she was smiling at a little boy sitting beside her. I took the photograph and studied the young woman's face. It was her – the witch.

'You used to be a nurse?' I said.

She nodded. 'A lifetime ago.'

'And the little boy?'

She didn't say anything, just smiled sadly.

'What's this?' I asked gently, pointing at the picture. She was wearing a badge – a sort of cross.

'It means I trained at St Thomas's Hospital,' the witch said. 'The Florence Nightingale School of Nursing. I gave it up, though, not long after that photograph was taken.'

'Perhaps that's why the nightingale sings when you whistle to him,' I said, smiling. 'He knows you're a nightingale too.'

'Ha.'

As I gave the photograph back to her I saw that someone had written something on the back: *1907, me and Moth*.

'Moth?' I said out loud. 'Is that you?'

'I suppose so,' she said. Then she repeated the word: 'Moth.' Her voice crackled like a flame and I couldn't tell if it was angry or sad.

As she sat in the darkness, with her fragile, white face illuminated by the moon and the faint glow of the fire, and her torn woollen wings folded around her, I thought it was a name that suited her perfectly. *Moth, the forgotten princess, banished to the dark forest . . .*

'I'm Henrietta Abbott,' I said, and I held out my hand towards her. She took it and gripped it firmly. Her hand was strong and warm. 'How d'you do?' I said.

'How d'you do?' she echoed strangely, as if the words belonged to a different language.

'And what's the cat's name, please?' I asked.

'Bright Star.'

I looked at the bedraggled little creature, and couldn't help laughing. 'He doesn't look much like a Bright Star.'

'Ha!' she replied, and for a moment her eyes shone. 'No,' she said. 'He doesn't, does he?'

I wasn't frightened as I walked back through the dark forest. *Robert would be proud of me*, I thought. *Perhaps I'm getting a little bit braver.* Somewhere high above me, a small brown bird fluttered through the treetops, watching me safely home.

13

Nanny Jane and I were having supper the next evening when something very disturbing happened.

Through the dining-room window, I caught sight of a shadow sweeping through the garden. My skin prickled. The brightness inside the dining room made it difficult to see, but I saw – or thought I saw – a shape near the trees. There was a sweeping movement, a glimpse of wings, perhaps. *An owl?* It moved again and I struggled for a moment to separate the shapes from the reflections on the glass . . . Then I saw it perfectly clearly. It was a ghostly figure, and it was walking, quite quickly, across our garden. I gasped and my hand flew to my mouth.

'Whatever is it, Henry?' Nanny Jane asked, staring

at me. She turned around to see what had startled me, but the figure had vanished.

'Are you all right? You look as if . . .' She faltered.

'I'm fine, thank you,' I said, swallowing hard. 'I just . . . I just thought I saw something.'

'Saw what, exactly?'

'Just a . . . an owl or something, I think.' My face burned.

'Oh. Well, there are lots of owls out hunting on these summer evenings, I should think,' Nanny Jane replied, smiling faintly. 'That's the countryside for you.' But there was a peculiar expression in her eyes as she looked away from me.

I woke early the next morning, and my bedroom seemed to be filled with the scent of roses from the garden. I thought of Mama straight away. Moth's words circled in my mind like a phrase from a song – 'There's bound to be a spare key to her room somewhere . . .' I went downstairs to the kitchen and inspected the hooks beside the back door. One key didn't have a label attached to it. It hung from a length of white ribbon and glinted in the morning sunshine, larger than the others and more beautiful, with an intricately patterned bow. I stared at it. Had it been there before? I didn't think so, but I couldn't be sure . . . Blurry half-thoughts of the elves and the shoemaker swam about in my half-asleep head – supernatural beings, characters from stories who visited houses while you slept . . . Then I remembered the ghostly figure sweeping across the garden and shivered. Something very strange was happening at Hope House.

I heard Nanny Jane's footsteps coming down the stairs and I panicked. I looped the ribbon over my head like a necklace, and tucked the key inside the collar of my nightdress. It hung there, cold as guilt against my skin. I breathed quickly. Nanny Jane's footsteps paused in the hallway, then went into the dining room. I pressed the icy key against my breastbone until it hurt. I knew exactly which door it would open.

I waited until after breakfast, when Nanny Jane took Piglet out for a walk in the pram. They were going to the village and back. It was Mrs Berry's day off, so I would have the house to myself. Nanny Jane would be half an hour at least. As soon as she had gone, I ran out into the garden and cut a single white rose. Then I sat on the bottom step of the stairs clutching the rose in one hand and my book of fairy tales in the other. I made myself wait for exactly three minutes. 'One Rumpelstiltskin, two Rumpelstiltskins . . .' I counted each second aloud, in time with the grandfather clock, until I reached one hundred and eighty Rumpelstiltskins. Nanny Jane would be well on her way to the village by now. I raced up the stairs and along the landing to Mama's room. I tried the door. *Locked*. My heart pounded, making the heavy key vibrate against my breastbone. I drew it out slowly from beneath my pinafore, pulling the ribbon. The key had been cold early this morning, but now it was warm from my skin – almost hot. It slid into the lock. I turned it slowly. *Click.* The door creaked open.

The room was flooded with sunshine. A million dust motes drifted in the light, and Mama was lying on her back, with the bedclothes pulled tightly across her chest. Her eyes weren't closed though – they were wide open, as if they were painted on – and her arms were straight at her sides. I was reminded of an Egyptian sarcophagus – and for one horrible moment I thought Mama was dead, but then she tilted her head towards me.

'I've come to see you, Mama,' I said.

She stared at me. 'You're not real,' she whispered darkly. 'I know you're not real.' Then, quite suddenly, her glassy eyes filled with tears.

'Mama,' I said. 'I'm real. *Of course I'm real . . .*' My eyes were full of tears too now. I didn't know what to do.

'Oh, you're *not*, you're not real,' she gasped. And then she was sobbing hard and a strange, agonized moaning came from her open mouth.

I ran to the bed and hugged her and stroked her hair and pressed my face to hers. 'It's me, Mama – it's your Hen – I'm here, I'm real, I promise.'

'You're here?' Mama sobbed faintly, and her whole body started to relax. 'You're really here. My Hen . . .' She breathed deeply a few times, smiled with relief and closed her eyes. A few moments later she was breathing steadily.

I placed the white rose on Mama's bedside table. I imagined her breathing in its heavenly scent while she slept, giving her sweet dreams.

She seemed to be falling into a deeper sleep now, although her eyelids fluttered like white butterflies and, sometimes, her hands moved in a similar, fluttering way. It looked so helpless.

'Wake up, Mama,' I said gently, holding her hands fast between my own. 'Mama?' Why couldn't she wake up? There was a bottle of pills on her dresser. A big jar with a bright yellow label: COMOBARBITAL – SEDATIVE. *Doctor Hardy*, I thought. *Doctor Hardy has given her these pills to make her sleep.* I wondered what Mama would be like now without the pills. Perhaps she might simply wake up, and be just like my old Mama again. But then I had a different thought: perhaps the real world would be too much for Mama now. Too much, and too empty all at once . . .

No, I couldn't let myself believe that.

I closed my eyes, pressed her pale, thin hands tightly and tried to pour all my strength into her. I thought of how I had felt when I heard the nightingale's song, and I tried to imagine its magic flooding from my fingers into Mama's. I wanted Mama to fight, not just for her own sake, not for Father's or even poor little Piglet's, but for my sake. For me. I knew it was a very selfish thing to wish, but I couldn't help myself. I wanted my Mama back.

Mama had read to me so many times when I was little; now it was my turn to read to her. I knew exactly which story I should read: *Little Briar Rose*, the Grimm brothers' tale of Sleeping Beauty. I knew every single word; I knew the patterns the words made in the air as they rose and fell together. I told Mama the story of the much longed-for princess, little Briar Rose, and the curse of the wicked old wise woman – that Briar Rose would die after pricking her lily-white finger on a spindle. As Mama slept, I told her about the deep sleep that claimed Briar Rose and every other inhabitant of the castle – a sleep that lasted for a hundred years.

My favourite illustration was on the last page of this tale – a view of the castle seen through the hedge of thorns. Through every window you could see the different characters fast asleep – cooks snoozing, dogs dozing, ladies-in-waiting, waiting to be woken . . . The prince was a silver silhouette in the foreground of this picture, dwarfed by the gigantic hedge of thorns.

I read the ending to Mama: the cruel hedge blooming into beautiful roses and parting before the prince;

his lonely walk through the silent castle; his discovery of the beautiful Briar Rose beneath a canopy of cobwebs . . .

I kissed Mama gently on the forehead.

And left her sleeping.

14

It was only the next day that I realized how confused Nanny Jane and the doctor would be when they found the white rose in Mama's room. I decided to sneak back in to retrieve it that morning, but I didn't have a chance. Nanny Jane had made plans.

Mrs Berry's husband, Archie, owned a pony and trap, and Nanny Jane had asked Mr Berry to drive us to the seaside for the day. Mrs Berry was given strict instructions on when to check on Mama and deliver her meals and medicine, and she gave us an enormous picnic basket filled with sandwiches, pork pies, sausage rolls and bottles of lemonade.

At about nine o'clock, the little old-fashioned trap rolled into the driveway, pulled by a sturdy brown pony. Down hopped Mr Berry. It was the first time I had met him properly. Nanny Jane had told me he had fought in the war and been injured. He had a stammer too, she said. Mr Berry hadn't worked since coming back from France. He just did odd jobs in the garden at Hope House and he usually brought Mrs Berry to work in the mornings and collected her each night. He nodded and smiled when Nanny Jane introduced me to him. Then he spoke to the pony very gently, stroking its thick, woolly neck.

'Steady there, Bert old boy,' he said.

I helped him heave the bulging basket into the trap and he added armfuls of the seaside things Nanny Jane had managed to assemble. The sea was walking distance from Hope House. From the attic window, it had looked like it would take about an hour or so, walking straight across the fields — but not with the baby, and not with all the paraphernalia Nanny Jane insisted on bringing . . . Mr Berry packed in the blankets, towels, changes of clothes, hats and bats and balls and painted tin buckets to make sand castles. I had no intention of making sandcastles. I wanted to stay at home. I wanted to see Mama again. I climbed up into the trap with what Nanny Jane called 'a face like thunder'. Unfortunately, the sky looked nothing like thunder — it was a deep, summery blue, strewn with fluffy white clouds.

Doctor Hardy arrived in his motor car just as we were leaving. Mr Berry's pony stamped and shied away

from the growling metal beast. Nanny Jane was locking the front door and she opened it again for the
doctor to go in.

'Not up to anything too exciting, I hope?' I heard
him say. 'The child really ought to be resting, like her
mother.'

'Just a quiet drive to the seaside,' Nanny Jane
replied steadily. 'I thought the sea air might do her
good. She can sit quietly and do a little . . .
embroidery.'

'Excellent, excellent,' he said. He patted his bulky
doctor's bag: 'I'll be able to carry out a few more tests
on Mrs Abbott while you're out.'

Tests? What sort of tests?

Then he lowered his voice and said something I
couldn't hear to Nanny Jane, looking straight at me as
he spoke. Nanny Jane nodded and looked straight at
me too.

'Perfect weather for a trip to the seaside,' Nanny Jane
said cheerfully as Mr Berry flicked the reins and we set
off.

'Where exactly d'you fancy, Miss?' called Mr Berry.
'A p-peaceful sort of spot or somewhere with
deckchairs and ice cream?'

'Peaceful, I think,' Nanny Jane called back (just as I
was about to vote for ice cream), 'though we'll need –
hygienic facilities.' She clutched Piglet tightly as we

turned the corner on to the road.

'I know just the p-place,' Mr Berry replied.

The drive took about a quarter of an hour. We trotted through the flat farmland – vast fields of crops on both sides and an enormous blue sky above. There was a breeze, and my hair blew around my face. I closed my eyes for a moment. We must have driven past a row of tall trees, as the sunlight flickered on my closed eyelids like a cinema projection. I breathed deeply, smelling the clean, salty air of the sea and, as we passed a field of cows, the warm, farmy smell of animal dung. I wrinkled my nose and Nanny Jane laughed. It was pointless sulking when Nanny Jane was determined to have fun.

I was imagining piers and promenades, brass bands, noisy crowds and the shriek of hungry seagulls. What greeted us as we climbed from the cart was something altogether more beautiful: a copse of pine trees, a little hotel, sand dunes tufted with blue-green grass, a broad white beach – and the sea. It shone like a jewel under the summer sun, stretching into the distance until you couldn't tell where it ended and the sky began.

I could just climb into a little boat, I thought, *and sail away for ever into that endless blue* . . .

'Until you bumped into mainland Europe, of course,' Robert's voice said, with his usual unforgiving logic. I smiled to myself. Further up the coast was the white lighthouse I had seen from the attic window, standing on the clifftop like a sentinel.

I helped unload the things from the trap and we all carried them over the sand dunes and on to the beach. Mr Berry went back to the cart for the picnic hamper.

'I'll be at the hotel, Miss,' he said to Nanny Jane as he helped arrange our things. 'Just let me know when you want to head home.' He smiled at me, and passed me a tin bucket. 'Have fun, little 'un,' he said.

Nanny Jane spread the blankets on the sand and we sat for a while, our faces turned up to the warm sun, listening to the gently crashing rhythm of the waves. Piglet lay on her front, like a little beached whale in a sun bonnet. She crawled to the edge of the blanket, grunting with effort, then collapsed and tried to eat a fistful of sand. While Nanny Jane cleaned her up and fed her something else, I took my shoes and socks off and walked down to the water. I was aware of Nanny Jane watching me and I sensed her desire to call out, 'Be careful, please, Henry,' but she just let me go.

It felt nice walking across the sand; I liked the way it moved beneath my bare feet, becoming firmer the closer I got to the sea. I edged into the water and allowed it to cover my toes. It was cold – startlingly cold at first, but I found that my feet soon became used to it and I paddled in a little further, tucking my skirt into my drawers. *Doctor Hardy wouldn't approve of this*, I thought with a grin. *No big adventures for small, bookish girls like me.* Presumably he thought I needed some sort of medication to cure me of my smallness and bookishness . . .

I gazed out to sea and breathed deeply, enjoying the feeling that I was part of the cold water and the clean air and the endless sky. I tried to let my thoughts drift through my mind as easily as the gulls wheeling high above.

I looked back towards Nanny Jane and Piglet to wave at them, and my heart jolted when I saw the dark silhouette of a man standing at the top of the sand dune, directly above them. It wasn't Mr Berry. There was something very odd about the way the man stood – at an awkward angle, perfectly still and staring out to sea. Was he aware that Nanny Jane and Piglet were right there, just a few yards below his feet, beneath his twisted shadow? He was leaning on a walking stick and, as I watched, he pivoted around and limped back towards the hotel. His stick shot out in front of him like an extra leg, and he moved surprisingly quickly, like an insect. Then I knew exactly who it was. It was the limping man who had called at Hope House the previous week – the one who had scuttled into my nightmares . . .

A colder current suddenly sucked at the sand beneath my feet and I lost my footing, falling back into the water with a splash – 'Oh!' I barely had a moment to catch my breath before a tall wave rolled towards me, folding down on itself and charging at me like a ram.

'Henry!' Nanny Jane shouted.

My face was underwater, and the freezing salt water filled my nose and mouth, blinding my eyes, burning my throat and driving the air from my lungs. I was lost in a splashing panic of grey-blue water and swirling skirts. But it was all over in a second. I managed to stand up, coughing, and lurched heavily towards the beach, my tears mixing with the salt water running down my face. I squinted up towards the hotel to see if the limping man was watching. Had he followed us from Hope House? But there was no one there now. It was as if I had imagined the whole thing.

Nanny Jane wrapped a towel around me and sat me down on the blanket. She dried my hair, wiped my eyes and gave me a glass of lemonade to take the taste of the sea away. She wasn't cross with me, and I was grateful. I blew my nose, then I unwrapped a paper parcel and ate a cucumber sandwich.

After a little while Nanny Jane said, 'It might be a good idea for you to take swimming lessons now we live so close to the sea, Henry.'

I dabbed at my ears with the towel; one of them was still filled with water and I couldn't hear properly. She sounded far away.

'I brought a spare skirt in case yours got damp,' she

added. 'Would you like to change?'

I looked at Nanny Jane's stern face, suddenly aware of just how lost I would be without her. She had started working for our family when Mama became pregnant with Piglet, though now it felt as if she had always been with us and I couldn't imagine our family without her. Our family. What had happened to it? We were just a few lonely people, held together by Nanny Jane's hard work.

I put my wet arms around her and kissed her cheek. 'Thank you,' I said.

Nanny Jane looked surprised and a bit embarrassed. She smiled, and then started singing 'Bonny Bobby Shafto' to the baby – it was one of her favourites.

It seemed a good moment to talk to Nanny Jane about Mama.

'Nanny Jane,' I began cautiously, 'can you tell me, please, about the medicine that Doctor Hardy is giving Mama?' And then the dam burst and all the questions just flooded out. 'And why doesn't he want me to see her? And what sort of treatment is he planning that needs Father's permission? And where does he want to have her admitted to? And—'

'Henry, stop – stop! I'm sorry, but I really can't discuss these things with you.'

Nanny Jane put Piglet down on the blanket and started tidying the picnic things. 'You simply have to trust that your mother is receiving the medical care that she needs.'

'But that's just it, I *don't* trust Doctor Hardy at all, and I don't *like* him either.'

'Henrietta! That's enough! You will show some *respect* towards your elders, please!' She was shouting now.

With fresh tears burning in my eyes, I picked up my socks, shoes and spare skirt, and walked up to the hotel to change. I stopped at the top of the sand dune and looked back; Nanny Jane was standing quite still, one hand over her mouth, looking out to sea.

15

Mr Berry drove us home in the trap later that afternoon. I turned my whole body away from Nanny Jane to stare out across the yellowy blur of fields, answering her questions as briefly as possible. Then I pretended to be asleep so I didn't have to speak to her at all.

Immediately after supper I was chivvied into an early bath and bed. Nanny Jane held out a spoonful of Doctor Hardy's nasty-tasting medicine. I didn't want to take it.

'I'm afraid Doctor Hardy has said it is necessary, Henry, particularly after such an eventful day,' Nanny Jane insisted.

She looked worn out and I didn't want another argument with her, so I took the medicine and got into bed. As my head sank into the pillow, I remembered the white rose I had placed next to Mama's bed. *Had it been found?* Well, it was too late to do anything about it now. Sleep was wrapping its soft tentacles around me and was pulling me down, down . . .

Nanny Jane was agitated the next morning. Her foot tapped a tattoo on the floor as she chewed distractedly on a piece of toast. Then she knocked the milk jug off the table. It smashed to pieces on the floor. Shards of white china trembled in a cool white puddle.

After I had helped clear up the mess, I asked if perhaps Mama could come outside and sit on the terrace with me for a while – it was such a lovely day. (Robert always used to say I was tenacious. I'd had to ask him what it meant: 'Hanging on to things, refusing to give up or let go . . . Like a tick,' he had said.)

'No, I don't think so, Henry,' Nanny Jane replied, without looking at me. 'Your mother needs to rest. Doctor's orders.' She collected up the last fragments of the milk jug and hurried off to the kitchen.

Doctor's orders. They had been law in our house since Robert's death. Why could no one else see that Doctor Hardy's orders were not making Mama any better? I wondered how long it would be before I would have an opportunity to visit her again in secret.

Just then, the telephone started ringing in the hall, as loud and urgent as the bell of a fire engine. I nearly jumped out of my skin. My tea slopped over the edge of the cup and spilt on my pinafore. I didn't move from my chair, though. I wasn't allowed to touch the telephone; it was one of Father's strictest rules. Robert had been allowed to answer the telephone in the London house on a few occasions, but only because he was older than me. I was rather afraid of it, to be honest – as if I thought I would be electrocuted if I tried to pick it up. I heard Nanny Jane's feet pattering towards it.

'Hello? The Abbott household?' she shouted. Then there was a long pause. When Nanny Jane spoke again, her voice was deliberately quiet, as if she was aware of me sitting there, listening. 'Are you absolutely sure this is necessary?' she hissed. 'I can cope perfectly well . . . No . . . No, of course not, but . . . Very well. Yes, I suppose so. If Mr Abbott has said that's what he thinks best . . . Wednesday, very well. And there's something else we need to discuss. Yes, exactly. I shall. Goodbye, then.' And she hung up the earpiece with a clatter.

What was that about? I wondered. But there was no point in asking. Secrets were growing quickly in the corridors of Hope House now. They were appearing overnight in fat, white clusters, like mushrooms in the dark loam of the forest.

Nanny Jane said she had to go to the village that afternoon to send a telegram. *To Italy?* I wondered. *To*

Father? Or was it something to do with that mysterious telephone call?

'I won't be long,' she said. 'Be a good girl, please, Henry, and help Mrs Berry prepare the vegetables for dinner.'

'Of course I will,' I lied. Beneath my pinafore, the key burned against my skin.

I read Mama the story of Rumpelstiltskin. It was not one of my favourites. I liked the brave miller's daughter, but I hated the stupid miller who bragged that his daughter could spin straw into gold, and the greedy king who locked her up and forced her to perform this impossible magic on pain of death . . .

But there was something about Mama's room that afternoon – a locked, lonely cell, with sunbeams shooting through the gaps in the curtains like spears of gold – that made me turn to that story. I read until the poor miller's daughter had married the king, and was begging Rumpelstiltskin not to take her baby – 'Oh, do not take her away!' The words hung strangely in the warm, dusty air of Mama's room, and I saw then that there were tears slipping silently from Mama's eyes and sliding down her colourless cheeks, like drops of wax down a candle. I held her hand tightly.

'It's all right, Mama,' I said urgently, my voice thick and choked. 'It's all right, I promise. Listen . . .' And I read that the queen guessed Rumpelstiltskin's name and won back her child. The story ended with Rumpel-stiltskin stamping so angrily that he drove his foot into the earth and tore himself in two. I didn't read this bit, though. I closed the book and finished the fairy tale myself, still holding Mama's hand.

'And so the queen kept her beautiful baby and promised her that she would never be taken away or locked up or asked to do impossible things, and that she would never, ever be alone.' I wiped my eyes on my sleeve. 'And they all lived happily ever after.' After a moment, I sniffed and added, 'Except the stupid miller and the greedy king who both died when a great big pile of gold fell on their stupid, greedy heads.'

Afterwards I sat for a while, watching Mama as she slept. The white rose I had placed on her bedside table had vanished. Someone must have taken it. *Nanny Jane?* Did she suspect that I had put it there? Was that why she had been in such a strange mood this morning? I would have to be more careful in future.

I caught sight of the clock on the mantelpiece: three o'clock. Nanny Jane would be back soon. *Just a few more minutes.* I took a brush from the dressing table and brushed Mama's hair very softly, teasing out the tangled ends one handful at a time and placing the tresses in shining coils upon the pillow. As I brushed, I thought about Doctor Hardy's treatment. Expecting Mama to get better all by herself, locked up in a dark and lonely room, was the same as expecting her to weave straw into gold, like the poor miller's daughter.

I stopped brushing. I suddenly felt quite certain that Mama needed to be rescued, and that I was the only person who could possibly rescue her. But what could I do? With Mama like this, we could hardly run away. No – I would have to find a way of defeating Doctor Hardy and his stupid doctor's orders right here at Hope House.

The first thing I needed to do was get rid of the pills.

I tried the drawer of her bedside table, the cupboard and the chest of drawers too, but everything was locked. Nanny Jane would be back any minute . . . Where else? I looked around. Mama's writing desk stood against the far wall. Beside it was a wastepaper basket – and in that was a single crumpled sheet of writing paper. I picked it out and smoothed it flat on the desk.

It appeared to be an abandoned first draft of a letter to someone called Doctor Chilvers. The date was the previous day – the day Nanny Jane, Piglet and I had gone to the seaside. It was not signed, but the address at the top of the page was Little Birdham Surgery. Doctor Hardy. Why was he writing to another doctor? I couldn't make out the meaning of it – the handwriting was so scribbled – but after squinting at the paper for a minute, a few frightening phrases became clear.

Rest cure is not proving sufficiently (something illegible) *for Mrs Abbott — advancing dramatically* . . . *Sleep cure* (something) *until admittance to* — here there was a word that looked like 'Helldon'.

Helldon? Was this the place Doctor Hardy wanted to send Mama to? And the 'sleep cure'? *That must be why he has increased the dose of her pills*, I thought. I wondered if Mama had dreams — or nightmares — while she slept. I wondered what it would be like having nightmares you couldn't wake up from. I shuddered and looked back at the letter. As I deciphered the final phrases, my insides turned cold.

Very interesting behaviour . . . (something) *possible emerging symptoms in the daughter too. Further observation required* . . . (This was where the ink had been smudged.)

The daughter?

Me?

Panic coursed through me. Did I have 'emerging symptoms' of something? I wondered what Nanny Jane could have told Doctor Hardy to make him think this. I thought about the strange looks she had given me recently when she had seen me talking to Robert, or when I had seen the figure in the garden . . . Perhaps I did have 'emerging symptoms' after all. My eyes moved over those last words again — 'observation required'. Who was going to be observing me? Doctor Hardy? Or this other man — I looked at the name at the beginning of the letter — Doctor Chilvers?

Then it clicked horribly into place, like the splintered ends of a broken bone pushed back together. The limping man. The limping man who scuttled like a spider, who had called at Hope House and who had been watching me at the beach. *He* was Doctor Chilvers and he was observing my emerging symptoms already.

Suddenly I felt dangerously alone. Mama was ill and drugged. Father was not here. Doctor Hardy thought I was going mad, and Nanny Jane had become his spy.

There was no one else I could trust. Except . . .

16

Moth was building a campfire, her back to me.

'Lend a hand, will you, Henrietta?' she said, without turning her head. 'Pass me those bits of wood.'

I took a deep breath and moved closer. I picked up a small dry log from a pile near the caravan and passed it to Moth.

'Fires are like living creatures,' she said. 'They have to breathe, and be fed.'

I swallowed and nodded, watching her.

She stood back and admired her work. 'Beautiful, isn't it?' she said. 'Like a sculpture.' She offered the box of matches to me. 'Go on,' she said. 'Light that twist of paper at the bottom.'

I shook my head and sat down on the steps of the caravan. Moth shrugged and lit the fire herself. Together, we watched the flames catch and grow.

'I need your help, Moth,' I said after a moment.

She laughed her short, dry laugh. 'Ha. My help.'

'It's Mama. She's sick. She's more than sick. I have to help her. And the doctor thinks I'm sick too — he's . . . observing me.'

Moth frowned and looked straight at me. She narrowed her eyes and her mouth twitched. 'Nothing wrong with *you*, Henrietta Abbott,' she said. 'Had a bit of a cold last week, but you're well enough now. You're as strong as a little ox.'

I felt a wave of relief. At least Moth didn't think I had emerging symptoms.

'Have you been able to see your mother?' she said.

'Yes.' My hand moved unconsciously to the secret key, hidden beneath my pinafore. 'Can you help her, Moth?' I asked. It came out in a very small voice. I took another deep breath and gave voice to the thought I had been keeping hidden, even from myself: 'I'm afraid she might die.'

Moth's smile faded. Neither of us said anything for a while. Bright Star nudged my knee with his cheek and sat down next to me. He folded his front paws neatly beneath his chest and looked up expectantly. I stroked his head.

'It's because of my brother, Robert,' I said after a

moment. 'He died last year. I think she is . . . I think Mama has been dying too, ever since. I have to help her.'

There was a pause while Moth thought about this.

'Yes,' she said. 'Yes. I see now.'

We sat for a while longer.

'I don't want her to be on her own any more,' I said, 'but it's like she's a prisoner now. And the pills Doctor Hardy gives her just make her sleep and sleep—'

'Yes. Yes, I know,' Moth said again, staring into the fire. 'I know all about him and his pills. As if sleep can cure grief . . . It's just one prison within another. It isn't sleep she needs. It's peace.'

'Peace, yes.'

'Your brother died,' she said, after a short while.

'Last summer,' I said.

'You miss him very much.'

'Yes,' I said. No one had thought to say that to me before now. 'Yes, I miss him every day.'

I waited to hear his voice in my head – saying something sardonic, but he remained silent.

'We used to argue a lot,' I said. 'He would snap at me and I'd snap back . . . It's the silence that's hardest to get used to. I feel like . . .'

Moth waited. *What did I feel like?*

'I feel like half a double act,' I said at last. 'I'm so sad he's gone. He was clever – good at numbers, at building things. He wanted to be an engineer like Father . . . I'm so sorry he didn't get to grow up and be a man and do all the wonderful things he wanted to do.'

The light of the fire danced in Moth's eyes. It was as if everything that was witchy and weird about her had just fallen away; she became more gentle, more real.

'A shorter life is still a life, Henrietta Abbott,' she said. 'I've thought about this a great deal. A shorter life burns briefly but brightly . . . A bright star.'

This made more sense to me than some of the other things I'd been told by well-meaning neighbours and vicars: 'He is in a better place now'; 'It was his time . . .' I turned the meaningless phrases over in my mind and felt the same blunt anger I had felt in those weeks after Robert's death. *A bright star*, I thought again, and a little of the anger melted away.

I remembered running with Robert through piles of leaves in Hyde Park on a sunny autumn day, both of us falling over and laughing so much we could hardly breathe. I thought about the way my imagination had conjured him here at Hope House – a voice in my mind, a shimmer of bright, golden light . . .

'*Bright Star* is the title of a poem by John Keats,' Moth said. 'A beautiful poem. A love poem.'

'I should like to read it.'

'He wrote *Ode to a Nightingale* too.' And she looked up into the trees above us. When she spoke again her voice was even softer. 'There is no cure for grief, Henrietta. But there is something that can lighten the darkness – just a little at a time – and that is life itself.

You know this already, I think. You know your mother needs stories, music, sunshine, birdsong, the smell of a rose, the smile of her daughter . . .'

'But the doctor, the pills . . .' I said.

Moth just nodded quietly. 'I know,' she said. 'But there will be a way to help . . .'

The sun sank lower and there was a moment of peace, as if the forest were holding its breath.

'The nightingale will sing soon,' Moth said. 'Whistle to him, Henrietta.' And she showed me how to make the soft, low sound.

I copied her. Nothing happened.

'It will come,' Moth said simply.

'I don't think so,' I said, staring up into the darkening branches.

'Try again,' Moth said. 'Listen for the things that can't be heard.'

I listened and listened until I could hear petals closing, clouds moving across the sky and tree roots creeping through the ground – then a very soft fluttering high in the branches above. My heart fluttered with it.

I lifted my head and whistled again – long and low. It wasn't an imitation of Moth this time, it was my very own sound.

And to my astonishment, the bird answered.

Moth smiled her crooked smile and I smiled back. We listened to the nightingale together.

'You see?' Moth whispered.

17

I was just coming down the stairs for breakfast a few days later when I heard the engine of a motor car growling into our driveway.

Nanny Jane was standing in the hall, ready to open the front door. I looked at her with raised eyebrows – *Are we expecting anyone?* Nanny Jane's eyes slid away from mine. Her face was closed. Her lips were tight.

I heard the sound of two car doors slamming loudly, almost in the same instant. Then I heard Doctor Hardy's voice and my heart sank. *Wait – two car doors? Has he brought the other doctor with him – Doctor Chilvers?* My heart fidgeted in my chest and I strained my ears to hear the voices drifting in from outside. But the second voice was a woman's.

Doctor Hardy strode through the front door, swiftly followed by an equally tall, grey-haired woman. She towered over Nanny Jane, who closed the door behind her. They all stood in a line, looking at me, and I stood there looking back at them.

The tall woman came forward.

'You must be Henrietta. I'm Mrs Hardy,' she said. 'Doctor Hardy's wife.'

Doctor Hardy's wife? What on earth was *she* doing here?

She stretched out a hand to shake mine. Doctor Hardy's hands were fat and crushing, but his wife's were cold and scaly, and her fingernails were thick, yellow claws. I felt as if I had just shaken hands with a giant lizard.

Nanny Jane was giving me one of her looks: *Manners, Henrietta!* I remembered the letter Doctor Hardy had written and his concerns about my emerging symptoms. Perhaps I ought to show him just how sane and reasonable I could be.

'How d'you do, Mrs Hardy,' I said, and I nodded and smiled at her husband. It was a particularly sane smile, I thought. 'Good morning, Doctor. Won't you both come in?' I said. 'Would you like some tea?'

'Charming!' Mrs Hardy said, and we trooped through to the dining room. Nanny Jane did not follow us; she went quickly up the stairs. I craned my neck to see where she was going. I did not want to be left alone with Doctor Hardy and his lizard wife.

Nanny Jane was only gone for a moment. She came straight back downstairs, but now she had Piglet in her arms. The baby was grumbling and rubbing her eyes. She did not appreciate having her morning nap interrupted, and I could not think why Nanny Jane would have got her up. Waking a sleeping Piglet was never a good idea.

Automatically, I reached out to take the baby from Nanny Jane, but she walked straight past me. Her face was pale and rigid. She plonked the poor, confused Piglet into the arms of Mrs Hardy and turned quickly away. 'I'll just ask Mrs Berry for some fresh tea,' she said, and headed for the kitchen.

Doctor Hardy had made himself comfortable at the end of the table, in Father's place. Mrs Hardy had taken the chair Nanny Jane usually used, with her back to the window. I offered them both some toast and marmalade.

'No, we've breakfasted, thank you, Henrietta,' Mrs Hardy said. 'Just tea for me, please. Black, no sugar.' And she smiled down at Piglet in her lap. It was then that I noticed the expression on her face. *Hungry* was the word I thought of. Mrs Hardy may well have 'breakfasted', but she was looking at Piglet as if she wanted to eat her up.

Mrs Berry brought in a large, steaming teapot and Nanny Jane followed with the cups and saucers. I noticed she had chosen the best china – the set painted with roses.

'Black, no sugar,' Mrs Hardy said again, although no one had asked. Mrs Berry poured tea for everyone and left. Nanny Jane sat down beside me, on the long side of the table facing the window.

Mrs Hardy was tickling Piglet's chin with a scaly finger. I saw the warning signs of a tantrum on the horizon. Piglet batted Mrs Hardy's hand away. She frowned and started turning crimson. Then she opened her mouth and let out a shrill, miserable scream. I stifled a smile. Piglet had excellent instincts about people, I thought.

'Oh dear,' said Mrs Hardy, standing up and putting Piglet over her shoulder. She tapped the baby's back in what she clearly imagined was a soothing manner. 'Oh dear, oh dear. You were right, Charles. She's not a happy little thing at all, is she?'

'What? Piglet? Not happy? Piglet's the happiest baby in the world!' I exclaimed, so surprised at her words that my own tumbled out rather aggressively. What did she mean by *You were right, Charles*? What had Doctor Hardy been telling his wife about my sister?

'I believe the child's name is Roberta, not *Piglet*,' Mrs Hardy said in a caustic tone. 'Honestly, the poor little thing! Spoken about as if she's an animal.' And she clutched the baby to her bony shoulder. Piglet screamed even louder.

I felt rage boiling inside me. Who was this woman? Who was this woman who didn't know my family at all and felt able to criticize us?

I stood up. I had no idea what I was about to say, but before I could say it, Nanny Jane's arm shot out and yanked me back down into my chair.

'Have some more toast, Henry,' she said curtly.

'And Henry?' scoffed Mrs Hardy. 'Henry is a boy's name. Henry and Piglet! I ask you! Your parents gave you both fine girls' names; you really ought to use them. We had our own little girl – Ruth. A beautiful child she was too. But the Lord took her before she was six months old.' Her eyes met Doctor Hardy's and I felt a wave of guilt for all the terrible things I had wanted to say the moment before. 'We are blessed with our sons, of course,' she went on. 'All grown-up now! Benjamin is the vicar of St Anne's in Ellory-below-Stave, and since dear Clarence returned from the war he has been working at Gibbons – that beautiful new department store in Norwich. He says he'll be managing the place by Christmas!'

'How lovely,' murmured Nanny Jane. She obviously felt something needed to be said in the pause while Mrs Hardy drew breath. Piglet, meanwhile, had got herself into such a state that she now brought up a little bit of milky sick on Mrs Hardy's shoulder. I tried not to laugh. I thought it was odd that Doctor Hardy wasn't saying anything. Then I realized why. He didn't appear to be listening to his wife at all. He was looking at me with a very serious, concerned expression on his face. Had he seen me trying not to laugh? *Perhaps I should say something . . .*

'How lovely,' I said, echoing Nanny Jane, and I stuffed a piece of toast in my mouth so I couldn't reasonably be expected to say anything else.

The Hardys stayed for another hour or so, during which Mrs Hardy tutted at my father's absence, pointed out the stains on my pinafore (tea, from when I had been startled by the telephone), said Piglet was far too plump, and finally suggested that Mama really ought to pull herself together for the good of her daughters. By the time the Hardys left, I was trembling with fury – ready to erupt. Why hadn't Nanny Jane defended us? Why had she allowed poor Piglet to go on squawking in that awful lizard woman's arms?

Nanny Jane closed the front door, an exhausted Piglet curled against her chest like a miserable pink grub.

'What was *that* all about?' I demanded.

'I'll thank you *not* to talk to me like that, Henry,' Nanny Jane snapped. 'And how dare you be so rude? It was simply a social visit from the doctor and his wife. She had expressed an interest in meeting you and the baby.'

There was something she wasn't telling me.

Simply a social visit? No, I didn't believe it. Doctor Hardy was up to something and – for some reason – Nanny Jane was on his side.

18

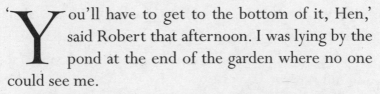

'You'll have to get to the bottom of it, Hen,' said Robert that afternoon. I was lying by the pond at the end of the garden where no one could see me.

I nodded, digging at the lawn with my bare toes.

'If you were a boy,' he said, in a thoughtful voice, 'if you were *me*, you would be "the man of the house" while Father is away.'

'I'm not a boy, though, am I?'

'No. But that's no reason why you shouldn't be the man of the house, Hen. *Someone* needs to be.'

He had a point. 'Do you think I should confront Nanny Jane? Do you think I should tell Doctor Hardy to go away and leave my family alone, and take his pills and his spies and his awful wife with him?'

Robert twisted his mouth to one side in that familiar way. 'That probably wouldn't be wise,' he said. 'You need to be clever about it, Hen . . . It's like David and Goliath. They're bigger than you, so you need to be cleverer. What do you know that they don't know? And what do you know that they know, but they don't know you know?'

'What?' I took a moment to untangle his questions. What *did* I know?

I knew about the secret attic room; I knew about Moth; I knew about the key around my neck, and the pills they were giving Mama, and Doctor Hardy's letter, and a place called Helldon. I knew that something was being plotted behind my back. I knew that they were spying on me. And if they could spy on me, I could spy on them too: I was very good at being unseen and unheard.

'Miss Henrietta!' Mrs Berry exclaimed as I entered the kitchen and sat down at the table. 'The very girl! Have a snack, dear.'

She plonked a jug of fresh lemonade in front of me and started cutting a wedge of bread from a newly baked loaf. I was just about to ask her if she knew the real reason behind the Hardys' visit when she suddenly said, 'Goodness! I must give this to you now before I forget.' And she handed me a very small parcel, done up in creased brown paper and frayed twine. It was addressed to me in an elegant, feminine hand.

Miss Henrietta Abbott,
Hope House,
Little Birdham

'Found it on the back doorstep,' Mrs Berry said, drying her hands on her apron and clattering about the place as she filled a large saucepan with water. 'Hand-delivered . . . Right little mystery, eh? Who do you suppose it's from?'

I walked to the back door and stood there in the sunshine, weighing the parcel in my hands for a moment before unpicking the tight little knot. The paper came away to reveal an old green book. It looked loved, like a child's threadbare toy. Golden letters spelt out the single word *Keats* on the spine.

I cradled the book in one hand, and allowed the pages to part and fall as they wished. They fell open at a poem called *Ode to a Nightingale*. I smiled my first real smile of that day. This book was a gift from Moth. I read the poem, whispering some of the beautiful words to myself: 'Light-winged Dryad . . . shadows numberless, Singest of summer in full-throated ease . . .' I didn't understand all of the words but I thought that I somehow *felt* their meaning. The poem seemed to be about escaping from sorrow – *yes* – that was what I wanted too. I drifted away into a daydream of forests and nightingales, and moths fluttering in the moonlight . . . I imagined the young poet, John Keats, in Nightingale Wood. He was lying on a great cushion of moss beneath an oak tree, staring up into the canopy above and listening to the nightingale's song. His face was as pale as the moon and his eyes, brimming with tears, were two bright stars . . .

Something startled me then – a loud, metallic banging noise – *one, two, three*. For a moment I was caught between my daydream and reality – was it a man swinging an axe – a woodcutter in the forest? *No, Hen, don't be silly.*

'Was that the door?' asked Mrs Berry. I closed the book of Keats, tucked it into my pinafore pocket and crept after her as she waddled out of the kitchen and across the hallway. She pulled the front door open and there he was – the limping man. *It must be him*, I said to myself. *It must be Doctor Chilvers – sent to observe my strange behaviour . . .*

I shrank back into the kitchen, afraid that he would see me. I could still see him, though. He was shorter than I remembered. His clothes were dark, smart and well-fitting. His face was very strange indeed – the skin stretched too tightly and pulled over to one side. His eyes were small and dark. A shiny hand gripped the top of his walking cane. He spoke very quietly and it was only from Mrs Berry's responses that I could follow the thread of the conversation.

'Yes, Jane said you'd call back . . . Yes, of course . . .

That's her, yes . . . She certainly did, I remember very well indeed . . . No, I'm sorry – I can't help you there . . .'

What is she talking about? Is she talking about me? I saw that the limping man was writing something down on a little notepad. Then he turned away as if to leave. Mrs Berry started to close the door, and I took a slower, deeper breath. The limping man frightened me horribly. He was spying on me. He was creeping around, asking people questions. I wanted him to go away and leave us all alone.

But then Mrs Berry called him back: 'Oh, now – wait a moment, sir! You should talk to Truman Pickersgill. He's the solicitor in Little Birdham – a nice chap. I do a bit of cleaning for him sometimes. He's in charge of leasing this house, you see, so he will know all about her . . .'

Solicitor? What would the solicitor be able to tell him about me?

'Pickersgill. Yes, the firm is Solomon and Pickersgill. Just off the High Street, Little Birdham . . . You're most welcome, sir. Good afternoon to you, too.'

I gripped the kitchen door frame tightly, waiting for the limping man to walk a little way down the drive. I felt like a fox must feel when the hound has missed its hiding place.

'Did he give his name, Mrs Berry?' I said, aware of a slightly hysterical note in my voice. If he really was

Doctor Chilvers, I needed to know.

She shook her head absently. 'No, I don't think he did, Miss.' She waved cheerfully to the village postman as he passed the limping man on the drive and approached the house. 'Afternoon post is it, Michael? Thank you!' She closed the door, passed the bundle of letters straight to me and waddled back into the kitchen. 'Have a quick look through, will you, Miss Henrietta? I need to hang out the washing . . . If there's anything for Nanny Jane there, will you take it straight up to her in the nursery? She said she's expecting something from your father.'

From Father? I felt a pang of jealousy that he was writing to Nanny Jane and not to me.

I shuffled through the letters and almost immediately found one addressed to Miss Jane Button. It was in Father's handwriting.

I needed to get to the bottom of things. I thought about what Robert had said by the pond: *You need to be clever about it, Hen . . .*

19

I waited until Mrs Berry had taken the washing outside, then went into the kitchen and looked around, my heart bumping guiltily against my ribs. Could I slice the letter open with a knife and reseal it so Nanny Jane wouldn't notice? No. I couldn't.

The kettle had started boiling on the stove. I picked up a cloth, lifted the kettle and set it down on the kitchen table so that the steam whistle wouldn't bring Mrs Berry back inside. I stood there for a second, the unopened letter in one hand, the warm handle of the kettle in the other. *Of course . . .*

'Whoops-a-daisy,' I muttered, smiling a little as I held the gummed flap of the envelope over the plume of steam escaping from the spout. 'I seem to have quite accidentally . . . steamed open . . . this letter.' The paper dampened slightly. I tried the envelope with my thumb, and it opened stickily. I bit my lip, stealing a glance out of the back door to make sure Mrs Berry was still busily occupied with the washing.

Dear Jane,

I hope you received my telegram in reply to your urgent message. I thought I ought to write to reassure you and clarify the situation.

Yes, I have given my permission for the Hardys to take care of the baby for a little while. I am sorry I did not get a chance to talk to you about this properly before Doctor Hardy's phone call.

I felt as if I had been struck in the stomach by a cannon ball. *What? The Hardys taking care of Piglet? No, please, no . . .* I remembered the telephone call I had overheard the other day, I thought about Nanny Jane's reluctant voice and her closed, rigid face during the Hardys' visit . . . Father had given permission for the Hardys to take Piglet away!

It is very kind of them to offer to help at this difficult time and it means you can dedicate more time to looking after Mrs Abbott while she is so fragile. Doctor Hardy has been highly recommended, as you know, and I feel confident that he and his wife will take excellent care of the baby.

I shall communicate further with Doctor Hardy

about the possibility of Mrs Abbott's admittance to Helldon. He seems convinced that it would be the best course of action.

I know Henrietta will be worried about her mother and sister. Please try to reassure her that these decisions are for the best.

Regards,
John Abbott

As if I were sleepwalking, I crossed the hallway, went down the corridor and into Father's study. I found some glue and resealed the envelope. It looked as good as new. While I had been steaming the envelope open it had felt like a game – I had been an actress playing a part in a moving picture. But it wasn't a game any more. It was horribly real.

I took the letter up to Nanny Jane in the nursery and handed it to her without looking her in the eye. I looked at the sleeping Piglet and briefly – madly – considered seizing her in my arms and running away with her – out of the house, down the road, all the way back to London . . . Instead, I muttered something about having a terrible headache, and tottered back downstairs. I felt as if a hundred bluebottles had hatched inside my brain and were buzzing blindly around inside my skull.

I gazed dumbly at my reflection in the hall mirror. The girl who looked back at me was a complete stranger. She was older than me, and thinner and sadder. She had dark circles around her eyes.

'Hello,' I said.

Her mouth moved but she made no sound. She stared helplessly at me, trapped behind the glass. I touched my fingertips to hers and watched as her face crumpled and she sobbed silently. *My whole world is being torn apart*, I thought. *And there is nothing I can do. Soon everyone I love will be gone.*

20

'For the last time, Henrietta – did you take my key and unlock your mother's bedroom door?' Nanny Jane demanded.

Doctor Hardy had been called and he stood there beside Nanny Jane, red-faced and quivering. He glared down at me as if I were a horrible little insect.

I looked Nanny Jane boldly in the eye and then glared back at Doctor Hardy too, just for good measure. 'I did not take your key,' I said. 'I don't know how Mama's door came to be unlocked this morning . . .' I thought about the key that hung secretly around my neck, beneath my nightgown, and hoped it wasn't visible.

Doctor Hardy tried a different strategy. 'I know it may seem cruel to keep her door locked, Henrietta,' he said, his voice dripping with something revolting instead of sympathy, 'but Mummy is not in her . . . She's not quite herself. She might easily fall down the stairs. We must do our best to look after her, mustn't we?' It was a dirty tactic.

'I understand,' I said flatly. 'I did not unlock the door. Honestly.'

Nanny Jane sighed with frustration. She clearly didn't believe me. Doctor Hardy rolled his eyes at her, and I saw red.

'I know what you're plotting, Doctor Hardy,' I said quickly. 'I know you're plotting to take Piglet away.'

Doctor Hardy laughed. He *laughed*. 'Plotting?' His saliva sprayed in my face.

Nanny Jane did not laugh. The expression on her face made me go cold. I swallowed with fear. I suddenly felt very small and stupid, standing there in my nightgown, throwing accusations at people.

'We will discuss this later, young lady,' Nanny Jane hissed. She and the doctor turned together and went down the stairs.

You idiot, Hen! I had done it all wrong. I had lost my temper. I should have picked my moment. I should have talked to Nanny Jane alone. I should have spoken calmly, rationally, like a grown-up . . . Like Robert would have done.

'Get dressed for the day, Henry!' Nanny Jane shouted up from the hallway. '*Now*, please!'

But I didn't want to. I went swiftly along the corridor and tried Mama's door. Locked again. I couldn't risk using my key while Doctor Hardy was still here . . . If I was caught, both he and Nanny Jane would be convinced that I was lying. I couldn't bear it.

I tried to think of the words I ought to use to explain my fears to Nanny Jane – but everything I could think of sounded childish and hysterical. I wondered if I should try to explain my Rumpelstiltskin idea – that Mama couldn't possibly get well while she was locked in a cell full of straw . . . *A cell full of straw?* My mind was getting so muddled . . .

As I stood there outside Mama's room, my heart still pounding with anger and confusion, I noticed that the low door to the attic room was not fully closed. I slipped through and crept up the stairs.

I sat down on the bed, tears running down my cheeks. I let them fall. Something wild surged up from deep within me and I wanted to roar with rage. I punched the mattress with a tight, white-knuckled fist. A cloud of dust billowed into the air. I was furious with myself for blurting out what I knew about the plans to take Piglet away, and I was furious with Nanny Jane and the doctor for making me feel like a criminal, for accusing me of something I hadn't done. I hadn't unlocked Mama's door in the night – *had I?*

Then I noticed something very odd. The attic was different. The long tendril of cobweb was no longer dangling from the ceiling. The model ships on the shelf had moved. A ship with a broken mast had somehow found its way to the little table beside the bed. My scalp prickled.

I got up and looked at the books by the window. *Moonfleet* lay open at the title page – the name A. Young was scrawled there in a clumsy, childish hand. *Is that the name of the little boy who once lived here?* I wondered, tracing the writing with my finger. *Is he part of this mystery somehow?* Then I saw that all the books had been rearranged neatly, in alphabetical order. *Someone has been in here. Someone has been creeping around Hope House while we are all asleep.*

Then a horrible thought struck me. What if it *was* me? Maybe I *had* unlocked Mama's door and crept up the secret stairs to the attic in the middle of the night . . . What if Moth was wrong and Doctor Hardy was right and I really *did* have emerging symptoms after all?

I stared out of the cartwheel window towards the sea, the key trembling against my breastbone.

21

After luncheon, Nanny Jane asked me if I wanted to walk with her to the village. Her manner was stiff and cool, but I sensed that she was sorry for our argument that morning. I agreed to go.

We walked along the verge at the side of the road in silence. Nanny Jane walked a few brisk paces ahead and I dragged behind, pulling at strands of grass and stripping away the dried seeds with my thumb and finger. I couldn't stop thinking about the mysteriously unlocked door, the model ships sailing spookily around the dusty shelves of the attic all by themselves . . .

We crossed over a river, and I stood on the stone bridge for a moment, gazing into the shallow water. The waterweed was thick and tangled, like the tangle of thoughts in my brain. This was the first time Nanny

Jane had taken me with her to the village of Little Birdham, but she had been coming here nearly every day – to post letters and send telegrams. I thought about Father's letter and the decision to send Piglet away. How many other decisions were being made that I knew nothing about?

Nanny Jane turned and looked back at me, frowning into the bright sunshine. She opened her mouth to call out, but stopped herself. Instead, she walked back to join me on the bridge.

'They're going to take Piglet, aren't they?' I said quietly, looking straight ahead at the river. 'Doctor Hardy and his wife.'

Nanny Jane didn't say anything for a moment, then she said, 'I'm not happy about it either, Henry. I have taken care of your sister since the day she was born.'

'Then why?'

'Your father thinks it's a good idea. So I can spend more time looking after Mama—'

'Whose idea was it?' I interrupted. 'Was it Father's idea, or was it Doctor Hardy's?'

Nanny Jane faltered: 'I think – I think it may have been the doctor's idea first. But your father trusts him completely.'

'Well, I don't,' I snapped.

Nanny Jane sighed. She did that a lot these days.

'It's not for ever, Henry – it's just for a little while. Until Mama gets better.'

'But she might never get better,' I muttered, feeling as if I were five years old. 'I don't think she will *ever* get better if she is drugged and locked in a room all by herself.'

'Henry, please—'

'And Mrs Hardy can't possibly look after Piglet – she's horrible. She's a horrible rude old – *lizard woman*.'

Nanny Jane's nostrils flared and she bit her lip, as if she were smothering a smile.

'Mrs Hardy may not be quite your cup of tea, Henry, or mine either for that matter,' she said at last. 'But she will look after your sister perfectly well, I'm sure.'

'But *I* can look after her,' I insisted. 'I'll be more helpful – I promise.'

'I don't think that's a good idea, Henry,' Nanny Jane said. And she seemed to be choosing her words carefully now. 'Doctor Hardy is worried about the effect your mother's illness is having on you.'

'What do you mean? It isn't having any effect on me,' I protested, confused.

'He's worried about you, and he doesn't think it's healthy . . .' She went on, 'He doesn't think it's safe for the baby to be in the house at the moment.'

'Not healthy?' I nearly choked on the words. '*Not safe?*'

'Henry, I'm sorry,' she said soothingly. 'This is awful for all of us. Please try to stay calm. Please try to understand that your father is simply trying to make the best decisions he can under the circumstances.'

My hands trembled on the railing of the bridge.

'Nanny Jane, what is Helldon?' My voice sounded very, very small.

Nanny Jane's head jerked towards me. 'How do you know about—' But then she inhaled and changed her tone. 'Don't worry about any of that, Henry,' she said. 'Nobody is going to Helldon.'

'But what *is* it?'

Nanny Jane tucked my hair behind my ear. 'Come along,' she said briskly, and she fished around in her purse. She found a coin and pressed it into my hand. 'Let's go and explore the shops. You can get some sweets if you like.' And she started walking again.

Little Birdham was a small village, in a sort of T shape, and the river curled around it like the tail of a sleeping cat. Two neat, white-washed little buildings stood in front of us – the post office and the village shop. Nanny Jane said she would go in to post some letters and send a telegram, then she had some shopping to do. I should meet her back on the bridge in half an hour and in the meantime I was free to explore.

Half an hour . . . A plan whizzed around in my mind, taking shape like wet clay on a potter's wheel.

I walked straight past the village shop, glimpsing all the brightly coloured jars of sweets in the window but resisting the temptation to go inside. I didn't have time for sweets today. I walked past a butcher's shop, a greengrocer and bakery, but by the end of the high street I had still not found what I was looking for.

I came to a junction and stood trying to decide which direction I should take. To my left the road appeared to lead to the village green. This, I thought, was where Doctor Hardy's surgery was. In the other direction, up a hill, I could see the church and a row of terraced houses. A white signpost read HAWKHAM. *Up the hill to Hawkham, or towards the village green?*

'Are you all right, my dear?' asked an elderly lady in a straw hat.

'Yes, thank you,' I said, smiling politely, and turned left. I stopped again almost immediately.

The door in front of me was painted bright yellow and had a knocker like the head of a lion. A brass plate bore the words SOLOMON AND PICKERSGILL, SOLICITORS. This was the place I had been looking for, the office of the solicitor to whom Mrs Berry had sent the limping man – Doctor Chilvers. This was my chance to find out more about him and why he was lurking around Hope House asking so many questions.

I knocked on the door. It swung open at my first knock to reveal a smartly dressed young lady sitting behind a desk. The hallway was quiet and smelt a bit like a library – paper, staplers and dusty carpets.

'Is Mr Pickersgill available, please?' I asked, trying

to make myself as tall as possible. I hoped I didn't look
– as I usually did – too much like a scarecrow.

The secretary smiled and her cheeks dimpled. I
couldn't tell if she was amused or simply being
friendly. 'I'll just check, Miss,' she said. 'Who should I
say it is, please?'

'Henrietta Abbott,' I said. 'We are tenants at Hope
House.'

The girl checked a large diary at the side of her desk
and then disappeared down the corridor.

I shifted my weight from one foot to another as I
waited. The floorboards creaked beneath the worn
carpet. A motor car drove down the road, then came
the clip-clop-rumble of a horse and cart. How much
time had passed since I had said goodbye to Nanny
Jane? Ten minutes maybe? I would need to be quick.

I heard muffled voices, and then a door closed
quietly. I was expecting a polite, 'Perhaps you could
come back another day,' or, 'Can I pass on a message?'
but the young lady reappeared and indicated the corridor behind her: 'First door on the right,' she said, and
turned back to the letter she was typing. 'Mind the step
down.'

22

Mr Pickersgill was browsing the bookshelves beside his desk, his hand moving across the books and files as if he were reading with his fingertips. He was a tall, skinny man, and he wore a creased grey suit that hung shy of his wrists and ankles, giving him the appearance of an overgrown school boy.

At last he found what he was looking for: 'Aha!' he exclaimed and turned to face me. A generous smile spread across his face. His eyes twinkled behind a pair of round spectacles.

'Miss Henrietta Abbott,' he said, stretching his large, freckled hand across the table. 'Truman Pickersgill. How d'you do?'

'How d'you do,' I said, wondering what a grown-up would usually say in such a situation. I added, 'Pleased to make your acquaintance, Mr Pickersgill.'

He smiled again and gestured to a threadbare old chair. I sat down.

There was an awkward pause during which I realized that, having asked to see him, I really ought to be the first to say something.

'It's a beautiful day,' I said.

'It is indeed,' he agreed, still smiling. 'I must say, it's quite a temptation to shut up the office and spend the afternoon pottering in the garden. Now, how can I be of help? I trust all is well with Hope House?'

'Oh, yes,' I said. 'I like it very much.'

'Good. Good . . . Perhaps you know that your cook, Mrs Berry, helps me out with a bit of housework from time to time,' he went on. 'She has told me a little about you.'

I wondered what she had said. Concern must have flashed across my face as he immediately added, 'About how helpful you have been with baking and so on . . . A dab hand at cake batter, so I hear.'

I nodded and took a deep breath. 'I don't suppose Mrs Berry has mentioned a strange gentleman who has visited Hope House?'

'She has not, but I believe I may have met the gentleman you mean. He paid me a visit this morning.'

'A man with a limp?'

'That's the fellow.'

My heart thudded. 'He has called at our house twice

now and I saw him at the seaside too,' I said. 'He's asking a lot of questions.'

'Yes,' Mr Pickersgill said. 'Yes, indeed.' I noticed his smile had changed. There was something more serious about it now.

'Can I ask who he is, please, and what exactly it is that he wants?'

He's Doctor Chilvers, my mind was whispering cruelly. *Perhaps he needs to get legal permission from a solicitor to have me locked away . . .*

Mr Pickersgill steepled his fingers and put them to his lips. He made a decision. 'I'm awfully sorry, Miss Abbott. I'm really not at liberty to answer those questions—'

'Is it to do with me?' I interrupted, aware that my voice was shaking.

Mr Pickersgill looked at me strangely. 'No,' he said. 'No, nothing to do with you, Miss Abbott.'

I studied his face. *Was he lying?*

'I can't go into any details, I'm afraid, but I can tell you it's to do with the family that owns Hope House. The Young family. The gentleman wants to get in contact with surviving members of the family.'

The Young family? I thought immediately of the attic room – *A. Young* scrawled inside the cover of *Moonfleet* . . . *But what does that have to do with Doctor Chilvers?*

'I arranged the Hope House lease with your father on behalf of the Young family,' Mr Pickersgill continued.

He tapped his chest a few times before he spoke again. 'I manage the property for them, you see. At least, I have done so since I returned from the war. My partner made the arrangements in my absence. Over the last few years, Hope House has been rented out to writers, retired couples and families just like yours. At one point the Catholic Church was interested in turning it into a convent, but . . .'

'But what?'

'I'm afraid nobody ever stayed for long.'

'Why not?'

Mr Pickersgill shrugged.

'Perhaps it's haunted,' I said, thinking of the books and ships moving around in the dusty attic room.

There was a pause. 'Nonsense,' Mr Pickersgill said, with an odd laugh.

'Was there a little boy?'

'Sorry?'

'The Young family — was there a little boy?'

'Yes,' he said after a moment. 'Yes, there was. Alfred.'

Alfred, I thought. *A.Young.*

'As a matter of fact, he—' Mr Pickersgill stopped himself. 'As a matter of fact, I really ought to be getting on with my work now, Miss Abbott. It has been such a pleasure to meet you. Goodbye.'

As I walked back through the village to meet Nanny Jane, I was aware of a strange kind of pressure in the air

— as if it needed to rain. I felt exactly the same pressure inside my head — a thundercloud was rising, swelling and threatening to burst. I thought of Piglet and Mama and Moth, of Robert, and John Keats, and a little boy called Alfred. I felt as if the weight of all these souls was pressing down on me.

It seemed that not everyone was prepared to follow Doctor Hardy's orders. While Nanny Jane was in the garden that afternoon, Mrs Berry called me quietly into Mama's room.

'See if you can coax her into eating a bit of soup,' she whispered.

Mama was sitting up in bed. Her eyelids were swollen and heavy and, as I came into the room, she smiled a slow, sleepy smile.

'Hen,' she said softly. I sat beside her and stroked her hand. 'I've missed you,' she said. 'Where have you been?'

I didn't know what to say. 'Exploring,' I said. 'Exploring the village, and the house, and Nightingale Wood.' I stroked her hand.

'Nightingale Wood,' she said, dreamily.

I managed to feed her a few spoonfuls of soup before her heavy eyes started to close. It looked as if she was trying to stay awake, but she couldn't fight it. *Doctor Hardy's pills*, I thought. *She wants to talk to me but the pills are making her too sleepy.* I remembered Moth's words – 'one prison within another . . .'

Mrs Berry and I helped Mama to lie down. I tucked the white counterpane around her.

Mrs Berry tidied up. Then she looked at her watch.

'Make sure your mother takes these with a sip of water, please, Miss,' she said, putting two round yellow pills in my hand. Then she picked up the soup bowl and left the room.

I stared at the yellow pills in my palm. I looked at Mama, sleeping like a china doll. I stroked her hair and sang Moth's strange song to her: 'Asleep . . . O sleep a little while, white pearl . . .' Mama smiled and muttered something softly.

When I heard Nanny Jane's voice downstairs, I left the room, taking the pills with me, buried in my tight fist.

23

The air that night was thick and thundery. I turned over and over in my bed, tangling myself in the sheets, desperate to find a cool spot on my pillow. When I did sleep, I dreamt the gigantic figure of Doctor Hardy was peering at me through my bedroom window – as if I were a doll in a doll's house. His wet, gleaming eye was the size of a carving dish. 'The man of the house?' the giant doctor boomed. 'You're not the man of the house! You're just a silly little girl!' He reached in through the window and tried to pluck me out of my bed with his fat, purple fingers. I ran on to the landing to discover that Hope House was on fire, and I woke myself up shouting out loud.

Later – it must have been after midnight – I was awoken again, this time by hurried footsteps up and down the landing, up and down the stairs. What was happening? My head still swimming with nightmares, I opened my bedroom door to find all the lights of the house blazing and Nanny Jane in a long blue dressing gown, her eyes wide with panic.

'Go back to bed, please, Henrietta,' she whispered when she saw me.

'What's wrong?' I said.

'Just go back to bed, please.' It was more urgent this time.

I looked past her, down the corridor, to see Mama's bedroom door standing wide open. 'Where is Mama?' I asked.

Nanny Jane pointed her nose at me. 'I am looking for her,' she said. 'She seems to have – escaped from her room . . . I've called for the doctor. Everything is all right, Henry. But you need to go back to bed right now.'

Then Piglet's voice wailed unhappily from the nursery. Nanny Jane closed her eyes and pressed her lips together. She turned quickly towards the nursery. '*Please*, Henry,' she said, 'I need you to go back to bed.' And she vanished inside. I heard her trying to shush and comfort the baby.

Nanny Jane's panic was infectious. *Where was Mama?*

I listened as Moth had taught me to listen, for the

things that couldn't be heard. My breathing slowed. I heard water cooling in the pipes, the house sighing with sadness and the moon sailing through the night. Somehow, I knew Mama was not downstairs, and I knew Nanny Jane would have checked the upstairs bedrooms and bathrooms. I walked swiftly and silently, straight to the secret door and climbed through.

It took a moment for my eyes to adjust to the gloom of the dusty stairwell. I crept up the stairs and then looked up, and stopped. I held my breath. The cartwheel window in front of me was alight with stars: it looked like a gigantic astronomer's star globe, lit magically from within. And standing in front of the window, staring out to sea, was a figure. A figure in a moon-white nightgown, her arms outstretched, her pale fingers spread like starfish. It was Mama.

I stepped closer, but she didn't notice me at first. She was transfixed by something that beamed in the distance, and cast a quivering path of light out over the black sea. The lighthouse. She watched the light as it swept back and forth over the waves.

'Mama,' I whispered softly. I didn't want to startle her.

She turned towards me then. She was awake – more awake than she had been for weeks – but her eyes were still glazed and confused.

'We need to tidy his room, Hen,' she whispered helplessly. 'It's my fault – I've been asleep for a hundred years . . . We need to tidy his toys away.'

She meant Robert. She thought these were Robert's things. She stumbled towards the bed and picked up the model ship with the broken mast. She tried to straighten it. She sobbed. I saw that a skein of cobweb was caught on her hair.

'Let me help you, Mama,' I said.

I took the boat from her very gently and used the hem of my nightdress to wipe the dust off it. Then I put it up on the shelf alongside the rest of the ghost fleet. We sat down on the bed and I brushed the cobweb from her hair. She smiled sadly through her tears. I couldn't tell if she really saw me or not. I couldn't help myself – I buried my head in her neck and hugged her. She sat quite still for a second, then she slowly put her arms around me. Tears ran down my neck and her neck too. I felt wet hair against my cheek and I didn't know if it was hers or mine. She held me tightly and I clung to her. The stars turned slowly in the cartwheel window.

I don't know how long we sat like that but, after a time, I heard Nanny Jane's voice on the landing below: 'Henry! Oh, dear God . . .' And her footsteps pelted down the main staircase to the hallway in a panic. I thought of my bedroom – just like Mama's – empty, with the door standing open. Poor Nanny Jane . . . I had to get Mama back to bed. I stood up and helped her to her feet. We made our way down the narrow stairs and into her room. I held on to her arm. How thin she felt, how light and fragile – like a bird.

I remembered what Moth had said about the things that might comfort Mama – little bits of life to lighten the darkness. So I talked to her quietly as I wiped her face and tucked the white counterpane around her, just as I had a few hours before. I told her about Moth and the nightingale that sang when she whistled, and the book of poems by John Keats. My voice seemed to soothe her, so I kept talking. I told her that, when she felt stronger, I would take her to Moth's home in the woods, and the nightingale would sing for us both. I described Moth sitting beside her fire – like a forgotten fairy-tale princess – with her wise, wild eyes and her pale face . . .

'Well, all this nonsense isn't going to help anyone.'

Doctor Hardy. He filled the doorway like an ogre, all bulging stomach and bulging doctor's bag. How long had he been standing there, listening? He opened the bag and took out a vial of liquid and a syringe.

24

'Not a good idea, young lady,' Doctor Hardy went on, as he prepared the syringe, 'filling up Mummy's head with that sort of codswallop.' He felt Mama's pulse and shook his head at Nanny Jane, who had also appeared, taking Doctor Hardy's place in the doorway.

'Where have you been, Henry?' she said. 'Was it you who unlocked your mother's door again?'

'No, Nanny Jane – I promise . . .'

'Then where on earth—?'

'Miss Button!' the doctor interrupted. 'Mrs Abbott needs quiet. Rest and quiet. She cannot be allowed to wander like this.' He shook his head again. 'Her pulse is absolutely racing.' He went back to his bag to rummage for something. I felt my pulse racing too. I sat beside the bed and held Mama's hand. She looked at me, and her eyes were clear and steady. Then she spoke.

'My nightingale,' she whispered.

The doctor and Nanny Jane both looked at Mama strangely.

'Delirious,' he said in a low voice to Nanny Jane. 'The pills can give some patients hallucinations . . .'

Nanny Jane manoeuvred me from the room and put me out on the landing as if I were a naughty cat. She closed the door. I immediately put my ear against it. 'I'm going to try a stronger sedative,' the doctor was saying. 'Her hysteria is bordering on psychosis, Miss Button. I'm afraid we will have to proceed with further treatment very soon. Doctor Chilvers is keen to start the experimental treatments.'

What experimental treatments? What are they going to do to Mama?

'Can we discuss this tomorrow, Doctor Hardy?' Nanny Jane replied. She sounded tired, anxious. 'I'm afraid it's been a rather long night.'

It was as if she hadn't spoken. 'We ought to press on as soon as possible. In the meantime you'll have to keep that one away from her . . .' *Me? Does he mean me?* 'Talking to her mother like that is not going to aid her recovery at all – it'll make her even loopier. I'll come over as soon as I've heard from Helldon to make arrangements for her transfer. Until then – absolute rest and silence, please. And for heaven's sake, keep

139

that door locked, Miss Button.'

I stepped away from the door as his heavy footsteps approached, but I did not have time to get to my bedroom. He ignored me anyway, bowling along the landing and down the stairs like a tweed-clad juggernaut, and strode out to his motor car in front of the house.

Nanny Jane emerged from Mama's room and locked the door behind her. *Helldon*, the doctor had said. *Helldon!* But Nanny Jane had promised . . . I waited for her to say something but she looked like she didn't have the strength. 'Come along, Henry,' she muttered. 'Straight to bed for you. I'm sure your mother will feel better in the morning. Doctor knows best.' And her words sounded oddly like a prayer.

'You won't let them send Mama away, will you, Nanny Jane? You won't let them? You said no one was going to Helldon . . .'

'Shhh, Henry,' she whispered. 'You'll wake the baby. You'll wake Mama.' And she steered me into my bedroom. 'What would your father say if he knew you .were up and about at this hour of the night?'

What would Father say? How I wished he was here to sort everything out . . . I climbed into bed and buried my face in my pillow. Perhaps if I thought about Father hard enough, with all of my heart and all of my imagination, he would hear me somehow, and it would work like a magical spell to bring him home . . . I managed to conjure his voice. Only his voice. He was reading to me from the chair by the window. Father had read *The Jungle Book* to Robert and me once when we were very small, and I had read it so many times since that I knew it almost by heart. Father was reading the part of the story where Mother Wolf saves baby Mowgli from Shere Khan the tiger — *her eyes, like two green moons in the darkness, facing the blazing eyes of Shere Khan. 'It is I, Raksha, The Demon . . . The man's cub is mine, Lungri — mine to me! He shall not be killed. He shall live to run with the Pack and to hunt with the Pack; and in the end, look you, hunter of little naked cubs, frog-eater, fish-killer — he shall hunt thee!'*

I saw the wolf and the tiger snarling at each other, their bodies taut, ready to fight. I felt the dry heat of the night, smelt the strangeness of the cave — an animal smell of damp fur and dried bone-marrow, the sharp-toothed breath of creatures that eat the flesh of others. I felt the fierce strength of Raksha's anger — the fury of a mother who is ready to kill, or die, to protect her young.

Half awake, half asleep, I felt my throat tightening painfully. If only I could protect Mama and little Piglet like this . . .

I woke up early, knowing exactly what I needed to do.

Still in my nightdress, I ran softly down the stairs and into the study. It was cold and dark in there. I opened the curtains and the room filled with saffron-yellow light.

I sat down at the desk, took a pen and a piece of writing paper, and began a letter to Father. I had the idea that I could perhaps find his address in Italy on one of the letters in Nanny Jane's room . . .

Dear Father,

I hope you are well and that your work is progressing smoothly. I am quite well too, although I am rather worried at the moment.

Was that the right word to use – 'worried'? I wanted him to know how troubled things were here at Hope House, but I did not want him to think that I was being hysterical in any way – I needed him to take my words seriously.

I have found out that Piglet is to be looked after by the Hardys, and this is of course very kind of them, but I do not feel that it is necessary, or the best thing for Piglet – or for any of us. Doctor Hardy is also talking about Helldon (is this some sort of hospital? They won't tell me), and experimental treatments for Mama. I am sure you know all of this, but I felt compelled [that was a good, grown-up word] to write and let you know that I am very concerned. I do not trust Doctor Hardy or his wife. Nanny Jane is doing her best but she is simply not . . .

And then a floorboard creaked behind me.

'Would you like me to post that for you, Henry?'

Nanny Jane asked. She was looking over my shoulder and her eyes were cold.

'No, thank you, Nanny Jane,' I said with a cheerful smile, doing my best to cover the letter with my arm.

'I think I'd better take it, don't you?' she said. It wasn't a question.

She reached beneath my arm, took the letter and scanned it – her eyes moving rapidly back and forth like the carriage of a typewriter. I felt a rash of heat spreading up my neck. It wasn't just what I had started to say about her that embarrassed me, it was my mock-adult tone, and the fact that my words exposed me as an eavesdropper, an envelope-steamer, a snake in the grass . . . Nanny Jane folded the letter in two and put it in her apron pocket.

'We don't need to worry your father unnecessarily, Henry,' she said. 'He has more than enough to think about at the moment.'

I nodded dumbly.

'Perhaps you could write to him about something else—' She was interrupted by the rolling crunch of tyres on the driveway. 'That will be the Hardys,' she said. 'I would like you to stay in here, please, Henry. You can use the time to think of something nice to put in a letter to your father.'

She left, closing the door behind her rather forcefully.

Something nice? What could I possibly write? I needed to

tell Father how dark and frightening things were here at Hope House . . . But Nanny Jane was going to check every word that I wrote. There was no way I could mention anything about Piglet or Mama or Doctor Hardy without her tearing it up and insisting I start again. Nanny Jane felt that I had betrayed her. Well, she had promised me that nobody would be going to Helldon. She had betrayed me too.

I was in a sort of trance now, staring helplessly at the blank page in front of me. I thought of blizzards, snow blindness . . . Then my hand picked up the pen and started writing again. But I didn't write a letter this time, I wrote a story – a fairy tale about a queen who had been captured by a wicked goblin called Despair. There was a witch in my fairy tale, and a moth, and a nightingale who sang from the summit of the Impossible Mountain . . . I looked at what I had written and my head sank into my hands. I remembered Father's words to me on the night before he left: 'You're too old for fairy tales now, Henry.' What use was a story? Stories couldn't change anything.

25

Muted voices were drifting from the sitting room.

'There was another case in the papers last month,' Mrs Hardy was saying. Even her voice sounded reptilian to me now – dry-mouthed and cold-blooded. 'A neurotic mother – poor thing – so confused after the birth of her twins that she drowned them both in the bathtub.' She sounded thrilled by the drama of this terrible story. 'Given the circumstances in this household and the severe condition of poor Mrs Abbott (my husband has told me about her delirium) – given these circumstances, I consider taking little Roberta under my wing as no more than my duty as a neighbour and a Christian.' She sounded very pleased with herself. I tried to picture her face and wondered if she was looking at Piglet hungrily again, as she had the other day.

I heard Nanny Jane's voice then – low, defeated: 'Well, all her things are in the bag, Mrs Hardy, along with clothes for the week and some of her favourite toys and books. Please let me know if you need anything else. She's generally an easy-going little thing.' I heard a well-timed grumble from Piglet, as if to prove Nanny Jane wrong. 'And please do let us know how she's getting along. Her sister is very anxious about this and we will all miss her terribly . . .'

'Her sister – well, she's another case *entirely*,' said Mrs Hardy.

There was the squeak and sigh of furniture as people stood up. A chair scraped on the wooden floor. I skipped a few steps backwards into the hallway, as if I had just left the study and had heard nothing of their conversation.

The door opened and out they came. The enormous Hardys, with Piglet wrapped up and ready to go out, clutched in Mrs Hardy's arms, and Nanny Jane behind them all, looking almost childishly small in comparison.

'Ah! Good morning, Henrietta!' said Mrs Hardy, her voice as piercing as the cry of a seagull. She looked me up and down. 'Not washed and dressed yet? My, my – we will need to do something about these slovenly habits, won't we?'

No, we won't, thank you very much ... 'Good morning,' I said, struggling to keep my tone civil.

'You can of course come to visit your sister whenever you like, Miss Abbott,' boomed the doctor. 'We aren't kidnapping her, are we, Mrs Hardy?' And they both laughed merrily.

My stomach was cramping and churning, and I fought back the angry tears that were swimming in my eyes. I walked straight to Piglet, looking only at her, as if she were floating in mid-air, and not in Mrs Hardy's arms at all.

'Goodbye, Piglet,' I whispered, kissing her forehead and her little turned-up nose. 'I love you and I'll see you very soon, I promise.'

Mrs Hardy took her out to the car.

Before he left, the doctor said he would check on Mama and give her a top-up of medicine. Nanny Jane didn't want me in the way, so she asked me to help tidy up the nursery and strip the sheets off the cot. I didn't like to disobey her, but I felt I had little choice. As soon as I heard the door of Mama's room closing, I crept down the corridor towards it. I needed to hear what Nanny Jane and Doctor Hardy were saying about Mama's treatment.

But they weren't talking about Mama. They were talking about me.

'I don't think she's lying, Doctor.'

'Then we have to consider the possibility that Henrietta is wandering around and unlocking doors in her sleep . . . All this time on her own, her mother descending into madness, her head full of fantasies – it just isn't good for her. Her behaviour really is very odd, Miss Button. You say it's just an active imagination – *I* say it's hereditary insanity – and Doctor Chilvers agrees with me. She is clearly developing some kind of serious psychosis just like her mother—'

Nanny Jane stopped him. 'I'm quite sure that isn't the case, Doctor. Really, she's just a little girl who has recently lost her brother. I'll keep a close eye on her and I'll look for—'

'After all,' he went on, talking over Nanny Jane, 'apart from the child, there really isn't anybody else it could be.'

'No,' she said. 'There isn't.' And I heard her sigh.

'Now, Miss Button, have you heard any more from Mr Abbott?'

'We exchanged telegrams yesterday.'

'And he said nothing about admitting her to Helldon?' There was a pause before the doctor spoke again. 'I'm afraid we *must* take the decision into our own hands. Her case has obviously worsened considerably during Mr Abbott's absence.'

'*Exactly*,' I thought I heard Nanny Jane say. 'If we could just *wait* for—'

'And so he does not fully comprehend the situation.

Miss Button, please try to understand that chronic cases like this require rapid treatment.'

'But don't you think she desperately wants—'

'What Mrs Abbott *wants* is neither here nor there. I am telling you what she *needs*. She must be committed if she is to receive the right care: intensive pyrotherapy, immersive water therapy, surgery if necessary . . . Doctor Chilvers is a genius – a pioneer in his field. Really, Mr Abbott should be honoured that Chilvers has shown an interest in his wife's case.'

Pyrotherapy? *Pyro* meant fire, didn't it? How could fire possibly help my family after what we had been through? And what was immersive water therapy? I thought about that day at the beach, and my panic as the cold salt water pulled me under, flooding into my nose, my ears, my mouth . . .

I couldn't breathe. I went to the nursery and stripped the sheets from Piglet's cot, just as I had been asked. I stayed in there, inhaling the sweet, baby-scented air until I heard the sound of Doctor Hardy's car leaving.

26

When I went into my bedroom that evening, Nanny Jane was there, rummaging through the drawers of the dresser.

'Can I help?' I asked from the doorway, making her jump. Her face went pink.

'I'm looking for—'

I knew exactly what she was looking for. 'A key? I told you. I promised. It isn't me, Nanny Jane! It really isn't!'

She looked at me for a moment and decided to change tack. She held up the book of Keats. 'Where did *this* come from?' she asked.

I should have said it was Father's. I should have lied, but I didn't. I didn't think quickly enough. 'Moth gave it to me,' I said.

She looked at me as if I really had lost my marbles. 'A moth?'

'Not a moth. Moth. She's my friend – a lady called Moth. She's a . . . a bit like a witch and she lives in the woods. She's very kind.'

I noted the expression that flashed across Nanny Jane's face.

'She's real,' I said defiantly.

'And this witch gave you a book of poetry?'

'Yes. I like poetry.'

'That's hardly my point, Henrietta.'

'What *is* your point exactly?'

Nanny Jane waved the book in the air. 'Witches in the woods? Talking to imaginary friends? Yes, I've seen you, Henry, I've heard you talking . . .' She looked at me closely. 'Is it – is it Robert you're talking to?'

I didn't say anything. I pressed my lips together and glared at her, determined not to cry.

'Henry, I know this has all been very difficult for you, very difficult indeed, but . . .' She took a deep breath. 'Doctor Hardy thinks you're sleep-walking. He thinks you're wandering around the house, unlocking doors without even being aware that you're doing it. He thinks your imagination is over-excited and—'

'I am *not* over-excited!' I erupted, painfully aware that I sounded very much as if I were.

'I believe it's very common to have imaginary friends – a whole imaginary world – when the real world is so difficult.'

'I am not imagining ANYTHING!' I shouted and, even as it flew from my mouth, I knew it was a lie. I snatched the book of Keats from her and stuffed it into my pinafore pocket. Furious tears were burning in my eyes now. I turned and ran down the stairs, through the kitchen and out into the garden. I hadn't unlocked the doors, *I hadn't*. Nanny Jane didn't trust me any more – she trusted Doctor Hardy and they both thought I was going mad.

I kept running and running, through the garden, through the trees, until I was deep in the middle of the wood.

Beneath an enormous oak tree I gasped for breath and cursed out loud and cried until I ached all over and had no more tears left. The sun was starting to set and, here in the shadows of the forest, a chilling dampness started to creep through the clammy earth and into my bones.

I looked around. I didn't recognize this part of the forest at all.

Was I anywhere near Moth's clearing? I couldn't detect even a hint of smoke in the air. I remembered that first day at Hope House when the smell of Moth's campfire had terrified me. How comforting I would find it now . . . I tried to remember the paths I had taken as I ran, but it was just a blurred chaos of trees and hot tears. I walked slowly now, scouring the forest for anything familiar. I listened as Moth had told me to listen, but the woods were silent and still. As I walked, Nanny Jane's words of doubt and accusation caught up with me, biting like insects.

Have I been sleep-walking? I thought. *Is it possible that I have been wandering around the house in the night, moving things in the attic, unlocking doors?*

I kept walking. I looked up at the ragged patches of sky and, deciding the pinkest glow must be to the west, I walked in the opposite direction, towards what I imagined must be the sea and, therefore, Hope House. But I came out instead at the edge of a long field. It looked as if it hadn't been farmed for years and was wild with meadow grass and flowers. A pair of rabbits turned and fled towards their burrows, their white tails bouncing through the twilight. At the edge of the field stood a tumbledown old house. The tiles were sliding from the steep roof and the windows were filthy. It had been abandoned long ago. The sign on the gate was hard to decipher, but some letters were legible and I decided it might once have said GAMEKEEPER'S COTTAGE. *Little Red Riding Hood's grandmother might live here*, I thought . . . Then I started thinking about blood-thirsty wolves hiding in the deep, dark woods. *What big teeth you have, Grandmother . . .* Trembling, I turned to face the trees again. I would have to go back into the darkness if I was to find my way home. Nanny Jane would be worried about me, especially after our argument. I remembered just how badly she had been affected by Robert's death, and now, in just one day, Piglet had been taken and I had disappeared too. Nanny Jane had lost all three of us. I needed to get home to her and Mama, but I couldn't bring myself to walk back into the woods alone . . .

The fading light swirled around the meadow, creating a shimmering, golden whirlwind. And I knew I wasn't alone any more.

Robert was here.

Part of my mind was whispering cruel taunts: *He's not real, Henry. He's just another one of your emerging symptoms . . .* But I felt better anyway. Robert was real to *me*. He wasn't a living, breathing person any more – I knew that – but he was still real. He was made out of the wildest, wisest, bravest bits of my imagination – my wild, wise, brave brother. And right now I needed him more than ever.

We stood there for a while, side by side, staring at the forest.

'You know what to do when you have to go into the darkness, don't you, Hen?' he said.

I shook my head. I couldn't go back into the woods. I had no idea where I was. What if I never found my way back out?

'You look the darkness right in the eye.'

'Yes?'

'And you run at it!'

'*Run?*'

'RUN. Ready?'

'No, Robert, wait—'

'One, two, three – RUN!' he yelled.

And then we were both running, hand in hand, pell-mell across the grass and into the trees, and I was yelling too, a fierce, fearless battle cry, and leaves whipped at our arms and faces, and the darkness reached out, but it could not catch us as we flew by. And then we were in the middle of the woods – and we were both breathless with laughter. *If only I could find the Robert part of me more often. If only I could be braver and wilder and wiser ...*

'They will be all right, you know,' Robert said as we slowed down to a walk, getting our breath back. 'Mama and the baby.'

'Do you really think so?'

'You can help them, Hen.'

'I can't even help myself, Robert. Doctor Hardy thinks—'

'Well, Doctor Hardy is wrong. You're Henrietta Georgina Abbott, and you're not just my little sister any more – you're a big sister now too. Remember that.'

'Yes.'

Robert led the way, stepping through the shadows of the trees. He turned back to smile at me as he became nothing but a shadow too, melting away into the darkness.

But I wasn't afraid. I was on a path now and, as I followed it, the trees started to thin out, the shadows turning from black to grey. I stepped from the leafy floor of the forest on to a harder surface. There were no trees at all in front of me.

It took me a moment to realize that I had somehow found my way to the main road. There was a roaring sound behind me then and I twisted around to see two bright lights moving towards me impossibly quickly . . .

27

There was a terrible screeching sound. The lights swerved violently and I threw myself back into the hedgerow, brambles scratching my arms and legs. The motor car roared past and then I was all alone again in the darkness and silence.

Silence? Not quite — I could hear a soft clattering and whirring. The clattering became the distinct clip-clopping of hooves, and I saw a familiar brown pony trotting towards me, pulling an old-fashioned trap.

'Hullo, there. Are you all right?'

'Mr Berry!' I shouted.

'Hullo?' Mr Berry called back. 'That isn't Miss Henrietta, is it?' He peered at me through the gloom as he pulled up the pony.

'Yes, I'm afraid it is,' I said, standing up and almost

crying with relief.

'A motor just came by me at a terrible pace and spooked B-Bert. Are you all right, Miss? I thought I heard a scream.'

Had I screamed? 'Yes – I'm all right. I just – seem to have got a bit lost, Mr Berry.'

'Well – what a b-bit of luck that I should run into you on the way to collect the wife from Hope House, then,' he said. 'No harm done, eh? Hop up, little 'un.'

I climbed up and, instead of sitting on the rear seat as I had done when he had taken us to the seaside, I sat beside him, relieved to be close to a kind body after the panic of the last few hours. We trotted towards Little Birdham.

'Well, now, how are you all getting on at Hope House?' he asked.

I didn't know what to say. I knew what the polite answer was – *'Everything is just fine, thank you'* – but I didn't think I was capable of telling such a lie. 'They've taken Piglet,' I said. 'Doctor Hardy has taken her.'

He was quiet for a moment. 'I heard as much,' he said.

'And they want to send Mama to Helldon.'

Mr Berry's brow furrowed. He concentrated on the road ahead.

'What *is* Helldon, Mr Berry? Nobody will tell me.'

'It's a sort of hospital, little 'un,' he said in a low, strange voice. 'A m-mental hospital. The old asylum up at Hawkham.'

The old asylum? Doctor Hardy wanted to have Mama locked up in the old asylum . . . I shivered horribly and my breathing became thin and quick.

'I was in there for a while,' he said. 'During the war.'

'*You* were?'

Nanny Jane had told me Mr Berry had been injured in the war, but that was all she had said. Now that I looked at him, I saw that there were scars – livid marks scored into his neck, his hands and one side of his face.

'You're wondering what happened to me, I expect,' he said. 'How I g-got these.' He touched the side of his neck.

I felt that I had been very rude for staring. 'I'm sorry,' I said.

'Not at all,' he said. 'Only natural you should be curious. Grown-ups always pretend not to notice.' He took a moment to steady himself. Bert trotted on down the twilit road. 'A g-grenade. Do you know what a grenade is?'

I said I did.

'My corporal got the worst of it. He was a good chap. I was the lucky one really – just caught a bunch of shrapnel, b-burst an eardrum . . .' He was silent for a second, then he said, 'Have a bit of trouble with my knee too, but that's from a knock I took earlier in the war. The B-Battle of the Marne – have you heard of it?'

I said I was sorry but I hadn't.

Mr Berry said nothing for a moment. Then he said, 'Ah. Well. We saved P-Paris that day.' Then, more quietly: '*Fluctuat nec mergitur.*'

'Is that Latin?'

'Yes. It's the motto of Paris — something like, *Tossed but not sunk.* The French translate it a bit more prettily — *She is tossed by the waves but she does not sink.*' Then he looked at me. 'We've all been tossed by the waves, haven't we, little 'un? The t-trick is not to sink . . .'

'*Fluctuat nec mergitur,*' I said. I smiled at Mr Berry and he smiled gently back. He twitched and rubbed at the scar on his neck. I was reminded of Father's burnt hand. *Scars on the skin only tell the beginning of the story*, I thought. *It's much more difficult to talk about the scars nobody can see.*

The doctor came early the next morning to do some sort of blood test on Mama, then he stayed for breakfast. He drank his tea in long, noisy slurps and spent a great deal of time mopping egg yolk from his bushy moustache with a napkin. He told us that Piglet was very well — that she had slept soundly and was demonstrating a healthy appetite. My heart ached jealously. I longed to have my little sister snuggled in my arms. I longed to kiss the top of her sweet-smelling, fluffy head.

'Can I come to your house today, please, Doctor Hardy?' I asked. 'You said I might visit my sister whenever I liked.'

He stared at me for a moment, a forkful of sausage halfway to his mouth. 'Of course,' he said, and shot a look at Nanny Jane. 'Perhaps this afternoon, Henrietta. I shall telephone my wife from the surgery so she knows to expect us. I'll pick you up around . . .' – he consulted his pocket watch – 'around three o'clock.'

After breakfast I was sent out into the garden so that the doctor and Nanny Jane could 'discuss things in private'. Looking back at the house, I saw him standing at the dining-room window. The doctor was watching me and appeared to be talking at the same time.

It felt very odd to be observed like this. I thought about Alice when she sees the Red King dozing beneath a tree and Tweedledee and Tweedledum tell her she is isn't real: she is just 'a thing' in the king's dream. It had always struck me as a terrifying idea, but now I felt it would be a tremendous relief. Soon the Red King would wake and I would melt away into the air, and the great weight of fear that pressed down upon me would melt away too.

Soon I heard the doctor's heavy footsteps crunching on the gravel, and I walked around to the front of the house. I know he saw me but he continued his conversation with Nanny Jane nonetheless: 'It really is an excellent institution. Doctor Chilvers has made some extraordinary progress experimenting with fever therapy. We must strike while the iron is hot, Miss Button!'

For a moment I imagined striking him with a hot iron, right in the middle of his bushy moustache. He kept talking to Nanny Jane as he clambered into his motor car: 'Be sure to tell Mr Abbott, won't you? Extraordinary new treatments! Cutting edge, cutting edge . . .'

28

At five minutes to three o'clock I was ready. I sat beside the study window, watching for Doctor Hardy's motor car. Nanny Jane had scrubbed my face and put me in my best dress. It was pale blue with a big lace collar. It was too tight under my arms. An edge of ribbon scratched at the back of my neck.

By seven minutes past three I was becoming impatient.

He's not coming, whispered a nasty voice somewhere at the back of my mind. *He's not coming. You'll never see your little sister again . . .*

Just when I was about to start ripping off the horrible scratchy dress, I heard the sound of a motor car. He was here. The study windows shook a little in their frames as the noisy engine vibrated outside the house.

'Goodbye, Nanny Jane,' I called, running out of the front door and leaving it swinging open behind me. Nanny Jane appeared in the doorway and waved as I climbed into the car. Suddenly I wished she was coming with me. I had no desire to be alone with the Hardys . . . What if they turned on me? What if they drugged me with yellow pills? What if they had invited Doctor Chilvers to tea to interrogate and examine me? Then I thought of the baby, clasped in Mrs Hardy's cold, scaly arms, and I remembered Robert's words – 'You're a big sister now . . .'

I had to be brave. For Piglet.

Doctor Hardy didn't say anything until we reached the junction in Little Birdham.

'Just a quick errand I need to do before we go home,' he said. 'It won't take long,' and he smiled horribly as he turned right instead of left. The motor car roared all the way up the hill, past the church and a row of houses, through a long tunnel of trees to a pair of cast-iron gates. The sign above the gates said just one word: HELLDON.

I felt a low, cold twist of fear. 'Why are we . . . ?' I couldn't finish my sentence.

'I just need to pick up some papers from a colleague,' he said simply. 'And I thought I'd let you get a glimpse of the old place. Your nanny says you're in a dreadful state about it all. It's not the least bit scary, you know!'

I stared ahead. I couldn't see a building at all, just trees and a winding driveway, like the skin of a dead, grey snake.

'Interesting fact for you, Henrietta,' Doctor Hardy said, in the manner of a know-it-all tour guide. 'The old asylums were built like this on purpose – with a curving driveway so you can't see the building from the main road. That's where we get the saying "going round the bend", because when you're carted off to the loony bin, you're driven round the bend!'

The loony bin?

'Let's go round the bend, shall we?'

I opened my mouth to protest, but I couldn't say anything. I couldn't breathe.

We bumped along the driveway, twisting first one way, then the other, following its unnatural, serpentine path. I did not want to see the asylum at all. I wanted to go home. Suddenly I was terrified that this was some sort of trap – Doctor Hardy had never intended to take me to see Piglet; he had tricked me into getting into his car so he could bring me to Helldon and deliver me into the hands of Doctor Chilvers . . .

'Here we are!' Doctor Hardy exclaimed.

And there it was. Helldon. It was a ghastly grey tomb of a building – square and ugly, four storeys high and dotted with tiny barred windows. I didn't look at them closely – I didn't want to see any faces looking back at me. I half expected to see Mama's face, some-how imprisoned behind one of those windows already, or the girl I had seen in the mirror — a thinner, older, madder version of me, silenced behind a dirty pane of glass . . .

Doctor Hardy stopped the car. 'See? Not spooky at all. Home sweet home, eh?' He climbed out of the motor car and called back to me, 'Just sit tight for a moment, please, Henrietta. I shan't be long.' And he entered the dark doorway of the building.

I panicked. *What if Doctor Hardy has gone to fetch Chilvers to lock me up?* Or was I just being hysterical? Perhaps this really was just an errand and he hadn't meant to frighten me at all . . .

There was a flower bed in front of the building, and a gardener was sitting beside it, pulling up weeds. I noticed that his right leg ended in a round stump at the knee, his trouser leg tied into a bunch with twine. A crutch lay on the grass beside him. *He must have been injured in the war*, I thought, *just like Mr Berry*. The gardener nodded at me and touched his cap.

'Don't want to hang around here too long, Miss,' he called out cheerfully. 'They might lock you up by mistake!'

I smiled weakly.

What should I do? Should I jump out of the car and run away? It was too late. Doctor Hardy was already heading back to the car, a sheaf of papers in his hand. I held my breath as he climbed in and turned the motor car around — slowly, painfully slowly — and I didn't breathe properly again until we were out of the driveway and on our way back to Little Birdham.

The Hardys' house was on the other side of the village, in a cramped cul-de-sac of new houses just off the village green. Their parlour was custard-coloured and stiflingly hot. It reeked of lily of the valley. Mrs Hardy had dressed Piglet in a frothy dress, all netting and bows — completely different from the simple clothes Nanny Jane usually dressed her in. The baby and Mrs Hardy were posed on the sofa together when we arrived, like a Victorian family photograph. I half expected Doctor Hardy to go and stand with them to complete the scene, one hand placed authoritatively on his wife's shoulder, but he disappeared into another room instead.

Piglet's face was beetroot red. She was either too hot or she had just had one of her tantrums. She held her little fat arms out to me as soon as I came in.

'May I hold her, please, Mrs Hardy?' I said, angry that I had to ask.

'Of course,' she said, with a thin smile, and passed her to me. 'It's nearly time for her afternoon nap, though.' Another wave of anger rippled through me. Mrs Hardy was enjoying this. This was a game to her. Well, I could play games too . . .

'She feels awfully hot,' I said, putting one hand on the baby's cheek, and I peeled off a woollen cardigan that was buttoned tightly over the frothy dress. 'I was reading in the newspaper about an old woman who accidentally killed her granddaughter by dressing her too warmly for this dreadful heat we've been having.'

I had read no such thing, but I wanted to hurt Mrs Hardy as much as she had hurt me. And I wanted her to know that I had heard all the sly things she had said to Nanny Jane when they took Piglet away.

'I'm sure she's quite well,' Mrs Hardy replied with a voice as cool as porcelain, but I thought I saw a flicker of concern on her face.

'Perhaps she has influenza,' I went on. 'There's an awful epidemic of influenza at the moment.' I had heard something about the high number of deaths from influenza in the past year, and I thought it could be useful ammunition. The Hardys would hardly want a sick baby in their home.

'She doesn't have influenza,' Doctor Hardy said decisively, strolling back into the room and sitting on the sofa next to me.

'Roberta is perfectly well,' he went on. 'And she has a new favourite game – don't you, Roberta?' He whipped Piglet out of my arms and balanced her on his knee.

'Humpty Dumpty sat on a wall,' he bellowed, 'Humpty Dumpty had a great fall!' And he bumped

Piglet down on to the floor.

Don't laugh, Piglet, don't you dare laugh . . .

I needn't have worried. Piglet had fixed Doctor Hardy with one of her most stern and unforgiving looks.

'All the king's horses and all the king's men,' – he was dancing her about like a reluctant puppet – 'couldn't put Humpty together again!' And he landed her back triumphantly on his knee. 'That was fun, wasn't it, Roberta?' he said in a silly high-pitched voice. Mrs Hardy was looking on proudly.

Piglet glared at him. Her face was perfectly stony.

I love you, little Piglet, I said silently, *I love you so much.*

I tried everything. I said Piglet kept the whole house awake night after night when she was teething. 'Oh!' I said. 'She looks as if she has another tooth coming!'

I invented a fictitious aunt – 'Aunt Susan', my father's sister – who was coming to stay with us, to help take care of Mama so that the baby could come home. 'I look forward to meeting her,' Doctor Hardy growled sarcastically.

Short of tucking Piglet under my arm like a rugger ball and running off with her, there was nothing else I could have done. In the end, quite desperately, I decided to try honesty. 'I miss her terribly,' I said quietly. 'And so does Nanny Jane. She is perfectly safe at home, I guarantee it.'

'I don't think you can *guarantee* that, Henrietta,' Doctor Hardy said, mocking my sincere tone. 'While your mother is so ill, the baby needs to remain with us.'

That was that, then. I had failed.

But only for today, I told myself as Doctor Hardy drove me home. I wasn't done yet.

My body ached with tiredness that night but my thoughts kept lurching and spinning in the darkness and wouldn't let me sleep. I struck a match and lit the candle beside my bed. I replaced the glass over the candle holder. I blew the match out and watched carefully until its glow had faded and died before putting it in the saucer.

The light of the candle flickered, and grotesque figures seemed to leap about in the shadowy patterns of the wallpaper. I lay down again, my mind torturing me with images of Mama lost in the dark corridors of Helldon. I was searching for her – I could hear her footsteps – but she kept disappearing around corners. When at last I found her, she was sitting alone in a white room. She had become Humpty Dumpty. Her skull was a fragile, shattered eggshell. Pieces of eggshell lay all over the floor and I was frantically trying to pick them all up for her . . . She kept telling me to leave the pieces and get out – the building was on fire, but I didn't listen until it was too late. I felt the heat on my skin, the smoke burning my lungs. I heard

Mama's screams — or were they my own? I forced myself to wake up.

I looked at the clock that stood on my mantelpiece. Midnight.

The witching hour.

29

I stood at my bedroom window and looked out at the dark shape of Nightingale Wood, hoping to see the familiar plume of woodsmoke rising from the trees; but there was no flicker of Moth's fire in the forest. I wondered where she could be.

And then I saw her.

She was in our garden.

It took me a minute to get outside. I could just see Moth standing beside the white rose bush, a dark shape against the shadowy forest beyond.

'Smell divine, don't they?' she said, gently pulling a rose towards her. The petals were loosely folded against the night.

'Like honey and oranges,' I said.

'Yes,' she agreed. Then: 'I saw the candle burning in your window, Henrietta. I came to see if you were all right.'

'I . . . couldn't sleep.' We stood together for a moment and then I said, 'Moth, they're sending Mama away. They're sending her to Helldon.'

Moth looked straight into my eyes. In that moment I saw all the way through her, through her crooked smiles and strange songs, right into her heart. I saw years of pain. She looked as if she was about to say something, but she just shook her head, and squeezed my hand in hers – warm and strong. A key swung from her fingers on a length of white ribbon. A key just like mine . . .

I thought about everything that had happened at Hope House in those past weeks – the books and ships moving around in the attic room, Mama's unlocked door. Then I thought of the photograph Moth had shown me, and the things Mr Pickersgill had told me about the Young family . . . I wasn't planning on saying anything out loud, but all these thoughts suddenly collided in my head and, before I could stop it, the question had flown out of my mouth:

'You're Mrs Young, aren't you?'

She looked at me for a moment, then she turned away and walked towards the mossy bench beside the pond. I followed and sat beside her.

'Who?' she said. I could tell she was bluffing.

'Mrs Young,' I repeated. 'You used to live here at Hope House.' I was reeling with the realization – and with relief: it wasn't a ghost, and it wasn't me – sleep-walking or going mad . . .

'Mrs Young? I haven't heard that name for years,' she said.

'But you are, aren't you?'

She gazed up into the night sky. 'I was once, but not any more, Henrietta. I am Moth now. You said so your-self when you saw the writing on the photograph. I'm just Moth.'

'I know you can help Mama,' I said. 'You know how to help her to get better, Moth.'

'All I know is that Doctor Hardy is wrong,' she said. 'With his pills, and his locked doors and his "rest cure" . . . He has no understanding of the human mind, or the human heart for that matter. I saw your mother one evening, just standing there at the window – so lonely and lost . . . I knew that feeling. I used my old keys and I went to her. I sat with her and held her hand and talked to her, so she knew she wasn't alone.'

Then I thought about the photograph again. 'You used to be a nurse, didn't you, Moth? If you can help Mama to get better soon, they won't lock her up . . .'

Moth shook her head. 'But I'm not a nurse any more, Henrietta.'

'You've helped me,' I said. 'The nightingale, and poetry . . .'

She smiled her crooked smile again. 'Poetry,' she said. 'That's about all I have left now. Just look at me. No poet ever wrote an ode to a moth . . .'

'They should have done,' I said. 'Moths are just as beautiful as butterflies.'

'No, they are not,' Moth said firmly. 'Butterflies fill the world with colour and light. The moth does not bring light — it is always in search of it. A moth is a cursed creature. I should know.' After a little while she said, 'Keats *did* write about a moth, as a matter of fact — a "death-moth" . . . *Ode on Melancholy* — have a look in the book I gave you.'

Moth had given me the book of Keats, and I knew now that she had given me the secret key too, so that I could see Mama against Doctor Hardy's orders.

'Thank you for the book,' I whispered, 'and the key.' I gripped it in my fingers like a talisman.

She nodded.

Then I said, 'I'm frightened, Moth.'

'Frightened?'

'Father is far away, Mama is lost, Piglet has been taken . . . It feels as if everything has been cut loose and has drifted. Everything has gone.'

'No,' Moth said, 'you mustn't say that.' And she thought for a moment, looking up into the night sky. 'It is just a new moon, Henrietta.'

I didn't understand.

'Even when the moon is just a thin white crescent,

the rest of the moon is still there, in shadow. It has not gone anywhere – we just can't see it. Look for the part of the moon that is hidden in shadow, Henrietta. Trust that it is there even when it can't be seen.' Her reflection shivered like quicksilver on the surface of the pond. 'It must be late,' she said. 'You should get back to bed now.'

'I can't . . . I'm afraid to sleep,' I said, thinking of the nightmare that had left me sweating with terror.

Moth drew a deep breath of night air into her lungs. 'Well,' she said, 'you'd best come with me, then.'

I watched Moth rebuild her fire and feed it with logs. It grew quickly and it wasn't until I felt its warmth that I realized how cold I had been. Moth gave me a hot drink that tasted of herbs, and then made me a nest inside the caravan – a great heap of soft, clean blankets to curl up in.

A little book lay on the table. I picked it up. It was a serviceman's bible from the war – the bible with the old picture inside. The photograph of Moth and the little boy.

'If you're Mrs Young,' I said carefully, 'then A. Young – Alfred – must be your son. The little boy who used to sleep in the attic room – with all his books and model ships . . . The boy in the picture.'

Moth stared at me and took the bible from my hands. She looked hurt, almost angry.

'I'm sorry,' I said. 'I didn't mean . . . I saw his name in a book in the attic. I didn't mean to pry.'

She sat down, holding the tiny bible between her hands.

'Yes,' she said, very quietly, 'Alfred was my son.'

'Where is he now?' I asked.

'Gone,' she said. 'The Battle of Jutland, 1916. Alfred joined the navy as soon as he was old enough to fight, but he never came home. The ship he was serving on was sunk and he drowned. He was still a boy really. Just a boy . . .'

'I'm so sorry,' I said, and I remembered what she had said to me about Robert – *a shorter life burns briefly but brightly. A bright star.* 'Did you go up to the attic room?' I asked. 'Did you tidy Alfred's things?'

Moth nodded. 'I needed to feel close to him again,' she said. 'You talking about your brother brought it all back. I never got to say goodbye, you see. I couldn't have a proper funeral. All those poor boys lost at sea and in the mud of no-man's-land . . .' The fire crackled outside the caravan. Moth squeezed my hand gently as she whispered, 'All our lost boys . . .'

30

Mr Pickersgill was busy, his smartly dressed secretary explained.

'*Please*,' I said. 'It's very important. Tell him it's about Mrs Young.' I had run all the way into the village straight after breakfast just to speak to him. I had to tell him about Moth. Mr Pickersgill had known the Young family, and he must have known that Alfred had died in the war, but I was sure he didn't know that Mrs Young was right there, living in an abandoned caravan in Nightingale Wood. My thoughts were excited and jumbled. I knew that Moth was somehow the key to everything at Hope House.

The secretary raised her eyebrows and went off to find Mr Pickersgill. I heard the low murmur of their voices. When she came back she said, 'He's in the old archive. End of the corridor, down the stairs. Mind yourself, Miss Abbott – it's a bit of a squeeze . . .'

It was a sort of cellar, and it was filled – absolutely jam-packed – from floor to ceiling with books, ledgers and files. They were stacked in great dusty towers on the floor and I had to thread carefully through them, as if I were deep underground, exploring a cave full of stalagmites.

Mr Pickersgill was sitting cross-legged on the floor in the far corner of the room, reading an old ledger by candlelight.

'Take a seat, Miss Abbott,' he said. 'If you can find one, that is.'

I carefully removed a pile of books from a wooden chair and placed them beside my feet. They weren't legal books at all, they were Sherlock Holmes stories. This wasn't just an archive, it seemed to be Mr Pickersgill's private library too. Suddenly I liked him an awful lot.

'Well, how can I help, Miss Abbott?' he said, twinkling at me through his glasses.

I couldn't very well talk about the weather this time. I straightened my skirt over my lap and took a deep breath. 'I need to talk to you about Mrs Young,' I said. 'I mean, Mrs Young of Hope House.'

The atmosphere in the cellar changed immediately. 'What exactly do you . . .?' Mr Pickersgill's question trailed off as his smile faded.

'You knew them, didn't you – the Young family?'

'Yes. My firm handled the sale of Hope House when Mr and Mrs Young first moved to Little Birdham – when their son Alfred was just a small boy.'

'What can you tell me about them?'

'Well, let me see . . . Mr Young was a wealthy man – family money, I think, but there was a problem with his lungs and he died not long after they arrived here. His wife had trained as a nurse and she looked after him all through his illness. That was nearly twenty years ago now. Mrs Young lived there at Hope House with her boy until the war. A wonderful woman.'

'I know,' I said, unable to contain my excitement any longer. 'I've seen her!'

Mr Pickersgill's mouth was open, as if he was about to say something but didn't know where to begin. He stared at me, his brow furrowed with doubt. I had seen that expression too often recently, from Nanny Jane, and Doctor Hardy too . . .

'I'm quite sure she's Mrs Young. She's –' I struggled to describe her – 'she's beautiful, and quite strange, and she's very kind. She lives in a caravan in Nightingale Wood – the wood at Hope House.'

Mr Pickersgill's face had changed again and I found it hard to read his expression as he interrupted me. His eyes sparkled dangerously. 'No, Miss Abbott, she doesn't.'

'She does,' I said. 'It's definitely her—'

He interrupted me again. 'Miss Abbott, I'm sorry . . .' He rubbed at his face, then he took a deep breath. 'Mrs Young died three years ago,' he said. 'She – took her own life.'

'What?' I didn't understand. The dark, dusty room started to spin before my eyes . . .

'She left a note saying that she couldn't go on,' he said in a low, steady voice. 'Then she rowed a boat out to sea in a storm, and drowned. Mrs Young is dead.'

31

Moth was Mrs Young. But Mrs Young was dead. It seemed that Doctor Hardy and Nanny Jane were right. I was losing my mind.

I tried not to notice Mr Pickersgill's expression as I apologized for wasting his time. What I saw in his face — and, I thought, in the face of his secretary as I left the office — was not impatience, anger or even confusion: it was pity. Were we the subject of local gossip, I wondered? *The crazy Abbott family — the mad mother, the mad daughter, the dead son and the father who ran away . . .*

Won't be long till she's for the loony bin too, the whispers seemed to say, as I hurried back past the post office, over the bridge and home to Hope House.

I wanted to run deep into the woods, to find Moth and curl up beside her fire in a nest of blankets. But I was scared that she wouldn't be there. And I was scared that she would.

When I got home I lied to Nanny Jane about where I'd been. I stood with the front door firmly behind my back, my heart banging like a battle drum. I resolved to put all thoughts of Moth and Mrs Young out of my mind. I thought about what Nanny Jane had said to me a few days ago when we had argued: *It's very common to have imaginary friends when the real world is so difficult.* Perhaps she had been right and Moth had indeed been part of all that too . . . I felt in my heart that Moth was real, but I knew now that she couldn't be – Mrs Young was dead. I tried not to think about the bizarre imaginary world that had almost swallowed me up like a great biblical whale. I wondered if all those strange goings on at Hope House really had been down to me after all . . .

That night I exhausted myself trying to sort what was real from what wasn't, but it was like untangling cobwebs. Perhaps that exhaustion was why I slept so soundly. My head felt clearer the next day. I woke up aware only of the empty nursery next to my bedroom and the locked door at the end of the landing. I needed to stop wallowing in worries and daydreams and stories.

I needed to get Piglet back. I needed to help Mama.

I was using my secret key to open Mama's door when I heard a floorboard creak heavily behind me. I froze.

Nanny Jane? This would make things a thousand times worse . . .

'It's all right, Miss Henrietta.' I almost collapsed with relief – it was Mrs Berry. 'It's all right,' she said again. 'Jane's nipped down to the village. Just you go along in and see the poor soul.' She smiled a firm smile. 'Don't seem right to keep you from each other. Just be sure not to tell that doctor . . . Well, go on, then – I've got to see to her bedpan and whatnot.'

I sat on the bed, next to Mama. She was sleeping deeply.

'They're going to send her to Helldon,' I whispered to Mrs Berry. 'Doctor Hardy wants to put her in the asylum.'

'I know,' Mrs Berry said quietly. Then, after a second or two: 'My Archie was in there for a while.'

I remembered the conversation Mr Berry and I had had in the trap the evening I had got lost in the woods. 'He said he was there for treatment during the war.'

'That's right. He was home for a while recovering from his shrapnel injuries. They were making arrangements to send him back to the front line when he started showing signs of what they're calling shell shock – shaking, panicking, that sort of thing. It's when his stutter started. Well, they put him in Helldon, patched him up God-knows-how, and sent him back. How he got through the rest of it I don't know. My husband was not a well man when he came home last year, Miss Henrietta, but he came home alive, and that's more than a lot of poor souls can say.'

'Yes,' I murmured. I wanted to hug her.

'There's a few boys still in Helldon,' she said. 'Being treated for shell shock. There's a doctor there . . .'

'Doctor Chilvers?'

'That's him, Chilvers. Fancies he's after the Nobel Prize or something. He gets up to all sorts in there. New treatments – scalding hot baths, surgery, giving folks tropical diseases.'

'Tropical diseases?'

She nodded. 'They inject you with a fever. Makes the body burning hot so's it does something to your brain. That's what it said in the paper. Chilvers thinks it can be used to cure all sorts of mental problems. Hardy worships Chilvers – wants to ride to glory on his coat-tails if you ask me.'

I was so shocked and frightened I could hardly get my words out. 'Do you think they'll be doing that to Mama – giving her a tropical disease?'

'Oh! Goodness – I shouldn't have thought so, Miss, no,' Mrs Berry said. Then she suddenly seemed to realize the implications of everything she had just said. 'Oh, Miss! Now, then – I didn't mean to scare you. It's probably all just rumours anyway. I'm sure your mother will be fine.'

But I had heard those conversations between

Doctor Hardy and Nanny Jane. I knew his plans . . .

'Here,' Mrs Berry said then. She unlocked a drawer and passed me a full bottle of Mama's pills. 'Be sure your mother takes two of these, and don't forget to lock the door again when you go. I've got to whip downstairs and rescue tomorrow's loaf from the oven.' And she left the room.

I couldn't believe it. A whole bottle of the dreaded pills had been placed straight into my hands. This was my chance. Without the sedatives, Mama would be able to wake up properly at last. Perhaps I could get up very early and take her to the caravan in the woods, so Moth could look after her and protect her from Doctor Hardy . . . I held the heavy bottle of pills in my hands.

There was a bang from downstairs. The front door. Nanny Jane was home.

'It's all right, Mama,' I said, kissing her quickly and saying goodbye. 'It's going to be all right.'

Then I tucked the bottle of pills under my cardigan and left the room, my heart thudding.

At midnight, I crept out to the garden and burrowed into the rose bed with my bare hands, scooping out a deep, dry grave. I dropped the bottle of pills into the hole and covered it up again, patting the earth down firmly and sweeping a deceitful layer of soil crumbs over the surface. Something danced madly inside me.

It felt like dark magic, like a pagan ritual. I felt as if I should say something – a spell or a prayer.

'Wake up, Mama,' I whispered. 'Wake up and be well again.'

32

'I want to help!' I had insisted. 'I want to help find her.'

I spoke firmly but inside I was a mess of terror. This was my fault.

Mama had gone missing in the night, and it was now nearly lunchtime. Doctor Hardy had organized a search party from Little Birdham. He had notified the police.

Nanny Jane told me to wait at home, but I refused. I got dressed quickly, pulling on an old, stained pinafore, and ran down the stairs.

I had woken Mama up with my spell. I had taken the sedatives away and I had forgotten to lock her door when I left. If I had given her the pills as I was told to, she would still be safely asleep in her bed. Then another thought occurred to me: perhaps Mama had heard the conversation I had had with Mrs Berry — perhaps she had not been asleep at all — and now she had run away, to avoid being sent to Helldon. For a moment I thought this was a good thing — Mama was free. But then I realized that I might never see her again, that Piglet might never see her again. I pictured her lost and frightened somewhere, wearing only her nightgown, her bare feet cut and bleeding.

We need to find her.

'We'll start with the woods and fields nearby,' said a young, pink-faced policeman.

There was a crowd gathered in the driveway of Hope House. Mr Pickersgill was there and a few other people I recognized from the village. Some, I suspected, were there for the excitement of it all. One man had brought his two dogs. They strained on their leads, eager to begin the hunt.

'Any volunteers to check the river?' asked the policeman.

The river? I felt sick. I had a horrid vision of Mama lying limp and open-eyed amongst the waterweeds . . .

I felt a hand on my shoulder. 'Come along, little 'un.' It was Mr Berry. 'D'you want to come and search with me?'

Bert, the brown pony, trotted through villages and farmland. The steady clip-clop of his hooves helped to steady my frantic heartbeat. I kept glimpsing white shapes moving at the edges of fields, in the cottage gardens. I would turn my head sharply, only to see the swish of a horse's tail or the fluttering of a sheet on a washing line.

'Where d'you reckon, then?' Mr Berry said. 'Where d'you think she'd go?'

For the hundredth time that morning, I racked my brains. We had checked the house from top to bottom. We had covered every inch of the overgrown garden. I felt that she might have gone into the woods, or to the meadow beyond, in which case the search party might well find her, but she had been missing for so long . . . She could be miles away by now; she could have walked all the way to the sea . . .

'Mr Berry, if you were to walk in a straight line from Hope House to the sea, where might you end up?'

'Pretty near that place I took you a while ago with your nanny, I should think,' he said. 'Or a bit further down the coast maybe – near the estuary – by the old lighthouse.'

The old lighthouse. I thought of the quivering path of light Mama had seen from the attic's cartwheel window. I thought of the way she had gazed at that light, rigid with emotion, her fingers spread like starfish . . . *They went there together*, I thought suddenly. *They stayed in the lighthouse keeper's cottage when Robert was a baby . . .*

'Can we try there, please?' I asked. 'The old light-house?'

'If you like, Miss. It's as g-good a place as any, I suppose.'

When Mr Berry turned the cart on to the narrow track that led to the lighthouse, I saw her immediately. She was standing near the edge of the cliff, looking out to sea.

An elderly man – the lighthouse keeper, maybe – shuffled about nervously a few paces behind her. He was holding a grey blanket in the same way that a bull-fighter might hold a red cape.

The sea breeze had turned Mama's nightdress into a white wind-whipped gown. Her hair streamed out behind her, wild and magnificent, her eyes were shin-ing. She looked like the figurehead of a ship, a mighty sea goddess – she looked *free*.

Mr Berry stopped the cart and I leapt out.

She is safe, she is safe. I started running towards Mama but there was the roar of an engine behind me, the screech of tyres. A car door opened and slammed.

'Get back, Henrietta!'

Doctor Hardy. Doctor Hardy was here.

And then another motor car appeared – a great black car – and two men got out. 'Get the child out of the way, for God's sake!' Doctor Hardy shouted. One of the men ran towards me. Before I could get any closer to Mama, a huge pair of hands had seized me, fleshy fingers digging cruelly into my arms. 'Put her in my car!' Hardy called to the man.

I fought with all my strength. My feet slid and skidded on the loose stones of the clifftop, my fingers tried to prise the hands from my arms. I heard a door open behind me and I was flung onto the back seat of Hardy's car. The door slammed shut with a clang. I was trapped. 'Keep her in there!' the doctor's voice yelled. The man did exactly as he was told, standing guard, imprisoning me inside the motor car.

'Mama!' I peered through the window, trying to see past my captor. Doctor Hardy was cantering heavily towards the edge of the cliff. I banged on the glass to warn her. 'MAMA!'

Hardy slowed when he was just a few feet away. He held something in his hands. A white coat? A leather belt? It was a straitjacket.

My wild breathing was steaming up the glass now and I had to wipe it with my hand so I could see. Doctor Hardy was creeping up behind Mama, the white jacket held open. I could see his lips moving but I couldn't hear what he was saying to her. It was as if I were watching a moving picture – there was nothing I could do to affect the events on the screen in front of me . . . I couldn't bear it.

'MAMA!' I shouted again, louder this time.

She must have heard me. She turned around and, at

exactly the same moment, the doctor lunged forward. Mama's mouth opened in a silent scream as she saw him, and her foot slipped backwards towards the cliff edge.

'MAMA!'

Doctor Hardy flung himself down on the grass and grabbed hold of her. I saw a flash of terror on his face – *his patient, he couldn't lose his precious patient . . .* There were other people helping too now – the lighthouse keeper and the other man who had come in the black car. They all pulled Mama safely away from the cliff edge. The strange man put her into the white jacket that Doctor Hardy had been holding. I could see Mama struggling. I managed to open the door a little and shouted again. She saw me and tried to come towards me, but Doctor Hardy steered her away. My captor shoved me back inside the car and slammed the door shut again. Mama tried to reach out towards me but the straitjacket held her arms down; she was sobbing and I was sobbing too, my hands flat against the car window – 'Mama!'

'Calm *down*, Henrietta!' Doctor Hardy shouted. 'You are really not helping anyone with this behaviour! Get in the trap with Mr Berry, please. We will see you back at the house . . .'

The man who had kept me prisoner opened the door at last. I watched helplessly as they put Mama in the back of the big black motor car, and drove away.

33

'Are you all right, Henry? How was your drive back with Mr Berry?' Nanny Jane asked, smiling at the air above my head. Something was strange about her. Her anxiety about Mama had been replaced with a brittle brightness.

'*Fine*,' I said, still shaken by the frightening events on the clifftop. 'I want to see if Mama is all right.' And I set off determinedly towards the stairs.

Nanny Jane took a step in front of me, blocking my way, and her face started to blotch with pink. Something was wrong.

'What?' I said. I tried to say it in a calm, grown-up way, despite the fact that my heart was beginning to bang painfully in my chest. 'What is it?' Then I said it again, almost shouting: 'What is it?'

Nanny Jane reached towards me with both hands and I saw that she was shaking. She opened her mouth to say something but no words came out.

I pushed past her and ran up the stairs.

'Where IS she?' I shouted.

Mama's room was empty, the windows open, the bed stripped of sheets. Doctor Hardy sat at the writing desk in her room, signing some sort of certificate.

'Now then, young lady,' he started, turning around slowly and removing his spectacles.

He was a blur. My whole body convulsed with each gasping breath. My throat was burning. I could barely speak. *Is she dead? Is she dead?* I heard Nanny Jane behind me in the corridor. I clung to the door frame.

'Mummy's not here, Henrietta,' Doctor Hardy said. Soothing, oozing.

I had never in my whole life wanted to strike anyone as much as I wanted to strike Doctor Hardy in that moment. My stomach was tight. My fists were tight. I felt Nanny Jane's hand on my shoulder and I nearly bit it.

'Mama's been taken straight to the special hospital,' Nanny Jane said. 'They left just before you got home.'

I could barely breathe. 'A trick!' I panted. 'You said you'd see me back at the house, Doctor Hardy – you made me think . . .' I glared at him. 'It was a trick! You've sent her away – to Helldon.'

'Now, then, young lady – you *did* know—'

'But I didn't say goodbye — you didn't let me say goodbye—'

'We thought it would be easier,' Nanny Jane said. Her voice was quiet, pleading.

'*Easier?*' I gasped, and my breath shuddered through me.

Doctor Hardy had turned back to his paperwork. I could read his mind — *No point paying attention to a child in hysterics. Best to ignore her* . . .

'We thought it was for the best,' Nanny Jane said. I could hear the doubt in her voice. I knew she was close to tears.

Doctor Hardy stood up. His chair scraped on the floor and he rustled some papers. 'There is a form here for Mr Abbott,' he said to Nanny Jane, booming quite deliberately, as if to dismiss my childish nonsense with his important business.

'I want to see Mama, Doctor Hardy,' I said, trying to control the tone of my voice. 'I want you to bring her home, please.' I looked straight into his eyes.

'Too late, I'm afraid — it's all official now.' He waved the form in front of my face and stabbed at the signature and date with a purple finger. 'Look!'

I stared at the piece of paper and tried to snatch it from his hand, but he passed it straight to Nanny Jane. 'Mr Abbott needs to sign too,' he said. 'Could you pop this in the post to him, please, Miss Button?' Then he turned back to me and bent his face towards mine.

'This isn't the Dark Ages, you silly girl – no one is going to lock Mummy up in Bedlam and throw away the key. She is quite safe in Helldon. Her doctors are highly skilled in treating such cases.' And as he stood up straight again, his eyes shone. 'Such extraordinary things they can do these days! Doctor Chilvers is delighted to have a female subject at last. He's terribly grateful to me. Female neurosis is a different kettle of fish from shell shock, obviously – so it opens up a whole new area of surgical research. He's really quite optimistic about her chances . . .' He squeezed past Nanny Jane with a gentlemanly bow and a flourish of his arms.

He seemed different, somehow – cheerful, excited. Mad Mrs Abbott was finally locked up in Helldon. The baby had been rescued from the dangers of Hope House. All was as it should be and *he* was the hero of the hour! I hated him. He had taken the fragments of my family, torn them into even smaller shreds, and scattered them in the wind.

He set off towards the stairs – 'A cup of tea, I think!' and then called back conversationally to Nanny Jane, 'I've heard that Chilvers may well be nominated for an award – if his current experiments are successful. How wonderful for me to be a small part of that! How wonderful for all of you too!'

How wonderful, Doctor Hardy.

I was numb.

I could feel how sorry Nanny Jane was, but I was too upset to even look at her.

I walked straight to my bedroom and stood at the window, looking towards Nightingale Wood. It was only then that I noticed the impossibly low, dark sky, and saw the tiny glistening drops clinging to the dusty window.

It was starting to rain.

34

It pattered evenly against the window. Steady, quiet rain. Then, without warning, there was a surge of sound, like ripping silk, and the rain poured down in a sudden, violent torrent. I tried to remember the last time it had rained – it must have been weeks ago . . . Time had been passing so strangely, I had lost track of what day it was. I thought of the date on the medical form Doctor Hardy had waved in front of my face. The pattern of numbers was familiar. Could that be right? The cogs in my head slowly turned around . . . and then the truth clunked into place. *It was my birthday.* How had I forgotten that *today was my birthday*? And everyone else had forgotten too – Nanny Jane, and Father. I had spent my birthday being held prisoner in a motor car on a clifftop, watching helplessly as Mama was taken away and locked up in an asylum . . .

Then another thought occurred to me: if it was my birthday, then it was almost exactly a year since Robert's death. I felt a cold wave of nausea. It struck me for the first time that I was catching Robert up – I had caught him up by a year already and it wouldn't be long before I overtook him . . . *How strange*, I thought, *how horribly wrong, to become older than my older brother* . . .

Dark clouds filled the sky now and the garden was nothing but a wet, black blur. But someone was there – a figure, the silhouette of a woman creeping through the dripping trees towards the house – *Mama?* Had she somehow escaped from Helldon and found her way home? I pulled the latch and forced the window up. I leant out into the storm and called, 'Mama! MAMA!' But she couldn't hear me over the rain. It was pelting down, drenching me. I would go to her. I turned back into the dark room. I crept on to the landing – it was vital that no one heard me . . . A floorboard creaked loudly, and then I was aware of something right in front of me in the gloom – I screamed and a monstrous face bellowed in reply. I bashed back against the door frame as the enormous creature lurched towards me.

'Good God, child! WHAT are you playing at?'

My heart was pounding so hard I felt sick. Doctor Hardy boomed again: 'What are you *doing*, Henrietta?' He gaped at me – my hair, my face and shoulders were dripping with rain. Had he heard me shouting? Did he think I had gone mad?

'Outside,' I gasped, 'to see Mama—'

'Mama? You weren't thinking of walking all the way to Helldon in this weather, were you? Your mother is safely locked up, Henrietta.'

'No – she's in the garden, she's—' And then I realized the mistake I had made. It wasn't Mama in the garden at all. I pushed my wet hands down into the pocket of my old pinafore, and felt something small and square and heavy – the book of Keats. 'Moth,' I whispered. 'It's Moth.'

'What? *Moth*? Miss Button, can you get any sense out of the child?'

Nanny Jane's face was a mask of fear.

'Henry . . .' There was a crack in her voice – she was close to tears. 'Not this witch-in-the-woods thing again, *please*. No more fairy stories . . .' She was crying now and so was I.

'She's *real*,' I said, gripping the little book tightly in my pocket. 'Moth's real – she's Mrs Young.'

Doctor Hardy's purple face loomed even closer to me. I thought I was going to vomit with fear. When he spoke again, though, his voice was cold, scientific. 'Mrs Young who lived here in Hope House, Henrietta? She is dead. She has been dead for three years.' The latter sentence was addressed to Nanny Jane, not to me. 'I was her doctor, Miss Button. I witnessed the coroner signing her death certificate at the inquest.'

'No, she can't be dead. She gave me this.' I showed him the book.

He seized my wrist. For a moment I thought he was going to drag me down the stairs to Helldon too – my arms were still bruised from where I had been held on the clifftop. I wanted to squirm but I forced myself to stay stiff and still.

Doctor Hardy continued to hold my wrist as he looked at his watch and counted under his breath. 'Fascinating, fascinating,' he muttered. 'Rapid pulse, delirium, hallucinations, somnambulism . . . I believe my initial diagnosis was correct: we are indeed looking at a case of hereditary lunacy. Most exciting! I shall speak to Doctor Chilvers about you, young lady, and we will make the necessary arrangements. But for now you need to get straight back to bed. And no more wandering around . . .'

He dropped my wrist, got a bottle of Soothing Syrup out of his doctor's bag and measured out a large spoonful of the foul black liquid. I shook my head. *No.*

'*Please*, Henry,' Nanny Jane begged.

I stared at her.

'*Please.*'

I opened my mouth for the spoon.

Nanny Jane moved me gently into my bedroom. As soon as the door closed behind me, I ran to the wash-basin and spat out the vile medicine. It swirled blackly against the white porcelain like a mouthful of blood. Then I heard a noise and spun around – the key was turning in the lock – they were locking me in!

'NO!' I slammed at the door with the flat of my hand and, outside, the rain slammed with me.

Doctor Hardy was talking, but not to me – to Nanny Jane.

'Absolutely not, Miss Button,' he said loudly. 'It would be foolhardy to allow Mrs Abbott to return home before her treatment has even begun. It is time to allow Doctor Chilvers to get to work. His methods really are at the cutting edge of psychiatric treatment—'

That phrase again – *cutting edge*. Scalpels, surgery . . .

Nanny Jane was protesting, still in tears: 'If we can just wait a few more days before starting treatment, Doctor. Mr Abbott says—'

I wanted to cheer. Nanny Jane was fighting for Mama. For a moment, even though she had just imprisoned me in my bedroom, I allowed myself to love her a little again.

But Doctor Hardy was adamant. 'No. We have waited long enough. It has been against all my instincts and principles as a doctor to delay her treatment for as long as this, keeping her here amidst all this – *chaos* . . . I am talking about her life, Miss Button! Her life!' And his heavy footsteps descended the stairs.

35

Lightning flashed and my room lit up, blue and white, then it was dark again, leaving only the blurred red echo of light on my eyelids. I lay perfectly still in my bed, counting the hours by the clock on the mantelpiece. Mama and I were both prisoners now. I felt as if something inside me had snapped. The ticking of the clock was the only thing that kept my heart beating.

Where was Robert's voice when I needed it most? Where was the shimmer of gold light? I clutched my book of fairy tales to my chest — as if stories could help, as if they held the answer somehow.

What could I do? The storm tore through the trees outside and thunder rolled around the sky like a colossal boulder. I thought of waves breaking fiercely on the shore, boats tossed on to sharp black rocks . . . I thought of the lighthouse on the coast, and the lamp lit by Grace Maskew in *Moonfleet*. And then I thought of Moth seeing the light in my window on the night I had found her in the garden . . . *Yes, a signal.* I would signal for help.

It took three attempts to light a candle – my hands were shaking. Finally the flame caught and I had a perverse instinct to blow it out again almost immediately, like a candle on a cake – *Make a wish. Happy birthday to me* – but I didn't. I placed the glass over the candle, and put the candle holder on the windowsill. And then I waited, and waited . . .

I must have fallen asleep. I dreamt the storm was inside Hope House: the walls shook with thunder, jagged lightning stabbed through the darkness and set fire to the curtains. And then I was back in London, standing on the street outside our house, watching violent flames pressing at the attic window. The window burst and shattered, someone screamed, black smoke belched out into the night and I heard the fire roar with satisfaction . . .

There were footsteps then, a key turning in a lock; a warm, strong hand taking mine. And then I was awake and we were running, running away from Hope House and my dream of the fire, and the London house, and Mama and Father, and Robert. Poor Robert. The storm was all around me as we ran, and it was inside me, too. The thunder vibrated in my chest and I felt the heaving of my brittle ribs, wrapped like frail fingers around my frantic heart. But I was still running some-how, the strong hand was pulling me on, through wet grass now, wet leaves on my face, the smell of wet earth and the rain pounding down on me. Something was bundled in my arms, something heavy and solid, wrapped in a blanket. My feet were bare and wet but they knew where they were going. *Somewhere safe.*

Inside Moth's caravan it smelt of dust and herbs and books. The cat was curled up beside my feet, purring. A lantern flickered on the low table next to the bed. The rain was a metallic clatter on the caravan roof, the thunder rumbled in the distance – the growl of a tiger that had lost its prey.

I was holding something heavy and familiar, wrapped in a damp blue blanket. I unwrapped it. It was my book of fairy tales.

'I saw your light,' Moth said. She was sitting there in the darkness at the other end of the caravan. She stood up and came to sit beside me. 'What did you bring to show me?' She took the book gently from my hands. She looked at it, turning the pages with care. She saw them all – those extraordinary, infinite worlds – enchanted forests, underwater cities, royal palaces . . . 'Beautiful,' she whispered. 'Beautiful.' She closed the book and rested the spine on her lap, her hands pressing the covers together. She smiled her crooked smile, then she moved her hands away and allowed the pages to part. It was my trick. She wanted to see where they fell open. I tried to stop her and reached out – '*Don't*,' I said. But it was too late.

We were inside the gingerbread cottage, inside the witch's oven – a great gaping mouth of fire. I felt, as I felt every night, when I forced myself to look at this picture, the burning heat on my face – the heat of fire and guilt. I was Gretel. My brother had been fattened for the oven and dragged from his cage. Now he would be killed and I had done nothing, nothing to save him. It was my fault. It was all my fault. It should have been me, not him . . . If I could just change the story – just go back – *please – can't I just go back? Make it so it never happened* . . .

But the flames of the oven were the faces of hellish demons, so horrible, they twisted and winked as I watched them. The coals glowed the colour of molten metal. The fire was so hungry – I knew I had to stop it somehow but I was too frightened and it was all too late – there was nothing I could do . . .

'Robert gave it to me,' I said.

'You can tell me,' Moth said, her warm hand on mine. She was watching my face. 'You can tell me the story of what happened to your brother.'

'I can't . . .'

She closed the book of fairy tales and gave it back to

me. 'Stories are powerful things,' she said quietly. 'And sometimes we have to be very brave to tell them.'

I nodded.

'Tell me what happened . . .'

So I did.

36

It began and ended with the moon.

The moon that night was huge and low in the sky. I stared at it until I felt I could reach out and touch its dusty white surface. I remember thinking it was like an eyeball, watching me, watching all of London . . .

I was hungry. I had been sent to bed without supper after arguing with Robert that evening. We were fighting more and more. *Soon there will be three of us, though,* I remember thinking – *and I won't be the youngest any more. The new baby is on its way and I will be a big sister.* I crept downstairs and helped myself to a chunk of bread and a glass of milk. I thought about waking Robert up to join in my feast – it was the sort of thing we used to do when we were a bit younger – but then I remembered the way he had spoken to me that evening.

I wasn't sleepy at all, so after my snack I decided to go up to the attic and read for a while in my comfy chair. I tiptoed along the landing, towards the attic stairs.

'You're supposed to be in bed, *Henrietta*,' a voice hissed from behind me. I nearly jumped out of my skin. I turned to see Robert standing there in his striped pyjamas, his arms folded across his chest, his frown just like Father's. He was still angry with me.

'And so are you, *Robert*,' I hissed back, climbing up the stairs to the attic. Those spiteful words were the last that ever passed between us.

They told me later that the fire had spread from the house next door – an oil lamp left burning in an upstairs bedroom. It was a clear summer night and I had curled up in my chair by the window to look at my brand-new book of fairy tales. The book had been my birthday present from Robert just the day before. I had never owned anything quite so beautiful. I thought about going back downstairs to say sorry to him, to make friends again. *Tomorrow*, I thought. *I'll say sorry tomorrow* . . . I remember reading the beginning of *The Little Mermaid* and gazing at the endless blue-green turrets of her underwater kingdom. I remember my eyes growing heavy and the fluttering of the curtains in the night breeze.

I was aware of something while I slept – a crackling and sighing like the warm breath of an animal. Then someone shouted my name and I was awake. I took in a lungful of smoke before I realized the attic was on fire. I tried to shout back but the smoke was like needles in my throat. I couldn't see. Someone shouted again – closer. I was feeling my way through the attic. I bumped into the corner of the table and immediately knew where I was. My feet found the top of the stairs and I felt my way down, away from the flames, away from the smoke, coughing and coughing, my eyes streaming.

Mama's arms were around me and I was safe. Nanny Jane was there. She pulled us both towards the main staircase – 'We need to get out – now! Outside – now!' But Mama wouldn't move, she screamed at Father: 'Where is he? Find him, John, for God's sake, find him!' Her hand was at her throat as if she herself were suffocating. Father ran from room to room.

'Up there? Was Robert up there with you?' He was shouting at me, but staring up into the burning attic.

'I don't know . . .' I couldn't stop coughing. Nanny Jane dragged me and Mama towards the stairs. Father yelled at us to get outside, and then we heard Robert's voice – above us – a distant, half-choked shout. That was when I understood the horrible truth. He had watched me go up the attic stairs. He had known I was up there. He must have fought his way through the smoke to find me — a brave knight battling a fierce dragon. A hero. And now, somehow, I was safe and he was lost. *It should have been me up there . . .*

I heard the bells of the fire engine and ambulance on the street outside. I heard a hundred voices shouting. Nanny Jane had got Mama out of the house but I clung to the bottom banister. 'ROBERT!' I shouted. Father plunged up the attic stairs but came back choking, he tried again and again until the firemen came and forced us all outside.

Father's tears cut rivers down his smoke-stained face. He had burnt his hand badly whilst trying to get into the attic and someone had wrapped it in a big wet bandage. Mama was beside him, big-bellied and help-less, sobbing through her hands. We watched the flames pressing at the attic window, then it cracked and shattered and more thick smoke poured out into the night sky. Flames licked through the tiles of the roof, something collapsed, the chimney shifted. We waited.

It felt like hours, but it couldn't have been very long at all. By the time the firemen put it out, the fire had devoured the attic next door, our attic and a large part of the roof. Everyone from the house next door had been safely rescued. As I stood there on the street, surrounded by strangers, I became aware that my birthday present, my book of fairy tales, was tucked safely under my arm. I had saved it from the attic. That was what I had chosen to save.

We waited for him. There was something horribly carnival-like about the anticipation of the neighbours crowding the street; the way they parted when he was brought out on the stretcher . . . I half expected a drum to start drumming for him, but there was only silence.

I remember the stripes of Robert's pyjamas, bright beneath the street lamp. I only saw his face for a second – his skin was alien-grey, like a sea creature scooped from its shell. In that moment, I knew he was dead. We all did.

Everyone saw him. The neighbours, the firemen, the eyeball moon . . . And everyone saw the moment in which my Mama broke. She was like a wild thing in Father's arms. I saw him try to catch her face to turn her away from the stretcher and she fought him like an animal. She broke free and ran, her long hair loose down her back. She reached for her boy and kissed and kissed his white hands as the stretcher disappeared into the ambulance. Then the ambulance man closed the door, and spoke quietly to her and Father.

The ambulance drove away, taking my brother with them, and part of my Mama too. It did not ring its bell.

How quick it all was – how final. Like surgery – the top part of the house was removed and Robert was amputated from our family.

*

I thought of the gardener I had seen at Helldon, and other poor men who had returned from the Great War with stumps instead of arms or legs.

Father had told me once that these amputees sometimes experienced feelings in their missing limbs — pain or an itch — and I thought about all those times I had seen Robert or heard his voice since he died: the aching I had felt for something that no longer existed. Was it the same thing? A part of my brain that couldn't accept that he was gone? Was it the last twitches of a sliced nerve — or was it just love?

'Perhaps that's what grief is, Henrietta,' Moth said softly, when I had finished the story. 'Grief is just amputated love.'

37

Moth tucked the soft blankets around me and blew out the candle in the lantern. 'You can sleep now,' she said.

I listened for the sound of rain on the caravan roof, but it had passed, and the distant thunder had faded into the night. The storm was over.

I was woken at dawn by the smell of bread toasting and eggs frying. Moth was cooking breakfast. We sat together by the fire. I ate and ate. The kettle boiled and Moth made sweet tea for us both. I had tried to think of Moth as Mrs Young, but I just couldn't make the name and the person fit together in my mind. I was quite sure she wouldn't want me to call her that, anyway. Mrs Young was a name for a normal grown-up and Moth was – different.

'Thank you, Moth,' I said as she passed me a tin mug of tea.

The cat emerged from the caravan, yawning and stretching his back legs, one at a time. Moth poured a little milk into a dish and he lapped at it greedily before settling down to wash himself.

I felt different today. Older. Lighter.

Then I thought about Mama waking up alone in the asylum, Piglet in the arms of Mrs Hardy, and a hollow space opened up inside me. I would sort it out. I had to sort it out. I would talk to Doctor Hardy and make him see reason . . .

'Doctor Hardy thinks I'm mad,' I said out loud. 'He thinks you're a hallucination.'

'Ha,' she said, and gulped down her scalding tea.

'Will you come and meet him? Will you tell him I'm not mad? Will you talk to him about Mama?'

'If he thinks you're mad, what will he make of me?' She gestured at herself – her wild, matted hair, her layers of old blankets . . .

'What about Nanny Jane or Mrs Berry?' I said hopefully.

Her eyes gave me my answer.

'But at least then they would know you are real. You are real, aren't you?' I said, biting into a piece of toast.

'Yes, I'm real,' she said sadly.

I took a deep breath. 'Mr Pickersgill said you took

your life. He said you left a note, saying you couldn't go on . . .'

'Ah.' Moth did not want this. But I felt we were close to some kind of peace now, both of us, and I desperately wanted it all to make sense.

She fussed around, piling up the empty tin bowls on top of some other dishes and the cooking pot. They wouldn't fit together. They teetered for a moment and then collapsed with a metallic clatter, shattering the stillness. We both jumped. The poor cat leapt up and sprinted into the trees, his eyes black with terror. A cloud of rooks took off from the surrounding treetops, creating a dark, squawking storm in the sky. Moth put her hands over her eyes and sat down. When she spoke again her voice was rough and strange.

'I couldn't go on without Alfred. I couldn't stay at Hope House. I couldn't remain in the real world. But it seems I wasn't quite ready for death either. Or he wasn't ready for me. One or the other.' She took a long, slow breath. 'I came here instead.'

'What about the boat?' I asked. 'Mr Pickersgill said you took a boat out into a storm . . .'

Without turning her head, Moth gestured towards the battered old rowing boat that stood outside the caravan, overflowing with herbs and flowers. 'Makes a lovely flower bed, doesn't it?'

I smiled.

'I believed my Freddie would come back,' Moth said

quietly. 'Even after I received the telegram saying he was gone. I thought about him out there in the cold dark sea, all alone. Doctor Hardy gave me pills to make me sleep. He said I needed to rest, but he was wrong. Drugged and all alone in that big house, I felt I was going mad. I started spending the nights out here in the woods instead, sleeping in the old caravan Freddie used to play in as a little boy. I lit a fire at night to guide his spirit home to me. One stormy night I realized I just couldn't bear to go back to Hope House. I wanted to disappear. You think I'm alone here, but I'm not. I have the trees and the foxes and the deer – I have the nightingale, and my cat, Bright Star. It has not been easy – it is never easy to give things up – but this is what I chose. This is my home now.'

'Everyone thought – everyone thinks you are dead.'

Moth looked me in the eye. 'Well, Mrs Young *is* dead. I'm Moth now. I'm free.'

'Yes.'

I thought about Mama then – standing on the clifftop, free, like a spirit of the ocean . . . And I thought of her wearing a straitjacket, locked in a cell at Helldon.

'Moth, I need to rescue Mama,' I said, and the words sounded so hopeless. 'It would all be so easy if I were a grown-up. People would have to listen to me then.'

'Ha. People don't always listen to you when you're

a grown-up,' Moth replied, smiling her crooked smile. 'But there are other ways, Henrietta. Sometimes, you can find a way of making people listen. And sometimes you can make things happen whether people are listening to you or not.'

As she spoke, a plan started coming together in my mind. I was going to have to be very brave. I was going to have to lie. And I was going to start by doing something I was definitely not allowed to do . . .

38

It must have been eight or nine o'clock in the morning by now, but Hope House was still asleep. Nanny Jane was usually an early riser. Perhaps she was exhausted from the events of the previous day, or perhaps Doctor Hardy had given her something to help her sleep.

I brought Moth in quietly through the kitchen door. 'This way,' I said, forgetting that Hope House had once been her home. I smiled an apology. We crept into the hallway. It felt very odd being here with Moth in broad daylight – I had always thought of her as a sort of nocturnal creature.

I picked up the earpiece of the telephone as I had seen Father do many times. My heart thundered as I imagined how horrified he would be at my disobedience. Moth looked around nervously. She pulled her blankets close.

'Hello? Could you put me through to Little Birdham Surgery, please,' I asked. Quite miraculously, the operator did exactly as I asked. I swallowed and took a deep breath. 'Hello, yes, this is Henrietta Abbott. Could I speak to Doctor Hardy?'

There was a click and a pause before I heard the doctor's sticky voice at the other end. He sounded angry at being disturbed. 'Yes, Miss Abbott?' he spat. 'And how are you feeling this morning?'

I spoke quickly, not giving him a chance to say anything at all: 'Doctor Hardy, thank you for all your help yesterday. I'm feeling much better, thank you. I just wanted to say that my Aunt Susan – the aunt I told you about when I visited the other day – has just arrived from – from overseas, and she would very much like to speak to you. She's here.'

I handed the candlestick part of the telephone to Moth and then the earpiece.

'Good morning, Doctor Hardy,' she said uneasily. 'It's – Susan Abbott here.' But then something started to happen. As Doctor Hardy spoke, the expression on Moth's face changed. She began to speak much more slowly, with a confidence I had not known she was capable of. Her eyes sparkled with something that looked like revenge. 'Yes, just arrived this morning from America . . . Well, to be honest I'm rather concerned about a thing or two. I've sent for my own nerve specialist from London to come and take a look at my sister-in-law as a matter of urgency.' She looked down at the script I had prepared. 'He's a highly respected chap – recently treated a member of the royal family, you know. He's very much looking forward to meeting you, Doctor Hardy . . .' I had told Moth how vain Doctor Hardy was, how ambitious. I knew he would be lapping up this sort of snobbish nonsense. I pictured his red face flushing even redder with self-importance. 'Yes, and your colleague too. Would you mind awfully telling Doctor Chilvers to hold fire on his treatments until my man arrives? You'll do that straight away? He'll be there no later than this evening, we hope. Many thanks . . . Yes . . . Oh, one more thing – please tell your wife I'll be popping over shortly to collect my niece. Thank you so much, Doctor Hardy. Goodbye.'

And she hung up.

'Thank you, thank you,' I said – it had been a magnificent performance. I flung my arms around her. Moth was rigid for a moment, and then her arms relaxed and she hugged me back warmly.

'Will you come with me?' I said. 'Please?'

But I already knew her answer.

'I . . . can't,' she said. She looked towards the front door and the world beyond Hope House with wide, wild eyes. 'I'm so sorry, Henrietta – I just can't.'

*

I put on my smart, going-to-church dress – not the blue scratchy one with the lace collar – a dark green dress with long sleeves that made me look older than twelve years old. *Thirteen*, my mind whispered. *You're thirteen now.* Then I walked to the village.

When I went into the Post Office to send the telegram, I tried to look as grown-up as possible. In my hand I clutched the coin Nanny Jane had given me to buy sweets the first time we had gone to the village together. I had done my sums: it would buy me just four words. They would have to be exactly the right words . . .

When the telegram had been sent, I walked through Little Birdham, past the village green, until I reached the cul-de-sac lined with elm trees.

I had thought to bring some flowers from the garden and had tied them into a bunch with a yellow hair ribbon. 'Gratitude can be disarming,' Moth had said. I thrust the flowers straight at Mrs Hardy as soon as she opened the door, dazzling her with what I hoped was a beaming smile.

'Good morning, Mrs Hardy,' I said. 'My aunt and I have come to collect Pig— Baby Roberta. Thank you so much for your kind offer to look after her – it really has been a tremendous help at this difficult time.'

'Your aunt is here, is she?' Mrs Hardy asked, snaking her head from side to side to see past me.

'Yes, Mrs Hardy, she's just waiting in her motor car around the corner.'

Mrs Hardy didn't budge. 'Well, I would have thought she might have come to introduce herself,' she said, her lizard mouth cold and tight.

'She sends her most sincere apologies, but we're late for an urgent appointment . . .' I had to clasp my hands together so she couldn't see how much they were shaking. This wasn't working . . . What was I going to do? I felt a cold, panicky sweat spread across my back. It was all very well trying to act like a grown-up, but this was a feeble performance. Mrs Hardy was not convinced for a moment. I considered giving up on the whole thing and running back home, but then a ray of sunlight caught the dimpled glass of the Hardys' front door. It shimmered like gold and I knew Robert was there beside me. His hand gripped mine. *Look the darkness right in the eye, Hen*, he whispered, *and RUN at it*.

'I'm so sorry, Mrs Hardy, but I really must insist on retrieving my sister,' I said confidently. 'My Aunt Susan is waiting.'

I gave her a diamond-bright smile, and pushed past her into the house.

Piglet was sitting in the middle of the living-room carpet wearing a silly frothy dress – all lace and frills. She looked like a miserable little meringue, but as soon as she saw me, she beamed and held out her arms.

I scooped her up and kissed her. 'Come on, Piglet,' I said. 'You're coming with me.'

'Well! I never——' Mrs Hardy blustered as I pushed past her again. 'What on earth do you——?' But she was too late.

'Don't worry about my sister's clothes and things,' I called over my shoulder. 'You can drop them off another day – whenever is most convenient. Thank you again – we're all so grateful!' And I gave her a cheerful wave as I walked swiftly down the path.

Did all heroes feel like this when rescuing fair maidens? Perhaps they did. I felt as if I was made of jelly. I held Piglet tightly and buried my face in her fat little neck as I walked, smelling her sweet Piglet smell and trying to forget all about the cold hatred that had burned in Mrs Hardy's eyes as she stood there, thwarted, on her own doorstep. Would she telephone Doctor Hardy to tell him what had just happened? Did she know that there was no Aunt Susan waiting in a motor car around the corner? Would she call the police? Was it still kidnapping if you were stealing back your own sister? There was no time to think about any of this now.

39

When we got home, Nanny Jane was sitting at the kitchen table with her head in her hands. She leapt up and her jaw dropped with surprise when she saw Piglet in my arms.

'Henry!' she cried, dashing over and holding my shoulders. 'I've been so worried – where have you been? Your room was empty – I've been looking everywhere!'

'I've been to get Piglet back,' I said simply.

'But . . . But your door – I locked it . . .'

'I can't explain right now, I'm afraid,' I said. If I told Nanny Jane I had been rescued by Mrs Young, she would not have believed me anyway.

'There's someone here who has missed you very much, Nanny Jane,' I said.

She was so overwhelmed to see Piglet, and Piglet was so delighted to see her, that Nanny Jane was quite incapable of saying anything else. She took her from me immediately. She helped her out of the ridiculous frilly dress and dropped it straight on to the kitchen floor. Underneath, Piglet was wearing a white vest and a cloth napkin. She looked like our Piglet again. The baby's eyes were locked on Nanny Jane's and she babbled intently, as if she were telling her a very important story.

I desperately wanted to talk to Nanny Jane too, to sit down with her at the table and tell her the truth about everything. 'There's something else I need to do,' I said instead. 'Keep Piglet here with you, Nanny Jane – no matter what Doctor Hardy or anyone else says.'

'No – Henry, wait—' Nanny Jane cried after me as I headed for the front door. 'Henry, you *can't* just—'

But I didn't stop. If I stopped now, it would all be too late. I didn't know if I had the strength to keep on being brave for much longer, so it was far better not to give myself a choice.

The walk to Helldon was a long blur of empty country roads and my own cold grey fear sweeping through me in long, nauseous waves. The sky had clouded over again and the whole world looked drained of colour.

I needed to get Mama out of Helldon, and I needed

to do it today. It would not be long before Doctor Chilvers realized that neither my Aunt Susan nor her nerve specialist existed, and he would start his experiments upon Mama. He would probably be very angry that I had tried to interfere. Perhaps the doctors already knew about my lies. If Mrs Hardy had seen through me, Doctor Hardy would now know the truth too . . .

The problem was that I had reached the end of my plan. I had no idea what I was actually going to do or say when I got to Helldon. I had started building a bridge without enough wood to complete it: I was about to walk right off the unfinished end and plummet into the icy water below.

I stood for a moment at the gates, looking down the long winding driveway of Helldon. I was half aware of a pony trotting along the road behind me, and I thought I heard someone call my name, but by the time I dragged my eyes from the hypnotic coils of the drive and looked around, there was nobody there. The road was empty. *You have to keep walking, Hen*, I said to myself. *You have to go on . . .*

I could not see the asylum yet, but I knew I was getting closer to that hideous tomb of a building with every step down the driveway. I thought of snakes and ladders. I had rolled the dice, landed on the wrong square and was now slithering helplessly towards my doom.

Helldon emerged slowly, sliding into view from behind the trees like a painted stage set. There was no turning back now. The main doors were standing open. *And welcomes little fishes in with gently smiling jaws*, I thought.

A nurse met me in the cold entrance hall. She held a bunch of keys in her hand. Her hat looked like the sail of a ship and she wore a pair of thick spectacles.

'Can I help, Miss?' she said.

'I'm here to visit my mother,' I said. 'Mrs Abbott.'

She walked to a desk in the corner and opened a large ledger. 'Mrs Abbott, admitted yesterday . . . Yes, she's in room four. No visitors, I'm afraid – for the time being at least.'

'But . . .' I started, and I fought the tears that were already starting to well in my eyes. 'If I could see her – just for a moment . . .'

Behind her thick spectacles, the nurse rolled her eyes. 'Wait here while I ask the doctor, please, Miss.' And she disappeared down a long dark corridor. I thought of the Minotaur's lair and wondered if I should have brought a ball of string with me.

I looked around. The entrance hall was cavernous. A wide staircase led up to the floor above. At the top, where the stairs met the first-floor landing, there was a high metal gate. A young man in pyjamas shuffled past the gate, muttering and shivering. A nurse guided him into a room and closed the door. *That must be where the patients are. Up there.* I looked at the gate and thought of Mama's locked door at Hope House, and then it was as if something finally woke up in my mind and I knew exactly what I had to do. The nurse had gone to ask a doctor if I could see Mama – that doctor was probably Chilvers. I needed to get Mama out before he could stop me. Something caught my eye on the desk in the corner. Next to the ledger, the nurse had left the bunch of keys.

I hurried up the stairs, taking care to be as quiet as possible. I fumbled with the keys, my fingers in a trembling panic. *This one – no – this one.* The biggest key fitted the lock of the metal gate, it clicked and the greased hinges swung open silently. The first floor smelt different from the floor below. It smelt of carbolic soap and something sharp and pungent – a caustic smell that reminded me of the science laboratory at my old school.

Room four – the nurse said room four . . . I glanced to my left and right. The corridors were deserted. *Left*, I thought. The floor was smooth and highly polished – in my hurry to find Mama, I nearly slipped. *Room six*, I saw . . . *room five* . . . And then Mama's door was in front of me. Locked. The smaller keys were numbered. Number four slipped through my fingers twice before I could grip it and turn it in the lock. Then I was there in her room and I saw her immediately – sitting up in a high narrow bed. She was awake.

'Mama!' I ran to the bed and put my arms around her. She was wearing a long green nightdress I hadn't seen before and, on top of that, the white straitjacket Doctor Hardy had put her in that held her arms tightly across her body. My fingers struggled with the buckles. My thumbnail tore.

'Come on, Mama,' I said, unwrapping the long sleeves and freeing her arms.

She looked at me and her eyes were huge with fear.

'Come with me, Mama. Hurry.' I took her hand. Her fingers were cold, white and bloodless. '*Please*, Mama . . .'

But she wouldn't move.

40

What could I say? What could I do? I couldn't drag Mama down the corridor or carry her down the stairs. I looked into her eyes again and a strange, frightened woman stared back at me. I knew Mama was inside there somewhere, lost in the dark maze of her mind just as we were both lost in the depths of Helldon. I had to reach her somehow . . .

'Let's go to the sea,' I whispered, remembering the look on her face as she had stood on the clifftop yesterday. 'To the lighthouse, Mama.'

Recognition flashed across her face. She looked helplessly towards the tiny barred window.

'No – this way,' I said. 'I'll help you.'

She took my hand and, very slowly, rose from

the bed.

We made our way together towards the staircase — shuffling and unsteady. We went through the gate and I locked it behind me, leaving the keys so I could use both hands to help Mama. Slowly, painfully slowly, we descended the stairs. One. Step. At. A. Time. Her eyes couldn't focus properly on her feet and she kept misjudging the depth of each stair. Twice I had to grab her thin arm to steady her. I thought dizzily of the attic stairs in our London house and imagined long fingers of flame reaching out for us as we descended. My skin prickled, every inch of me was burning, listening for voices or footsteps, but everything was eerily quiet. Was it some sort of trap?

'Nearly there, Mama,' I whispered, and our feet finally met the stone floor of the entrance hall. She shivered. She looked almost childlike in that baggy green nightdress — I cursed myself for not bringing spare clothes or shoes for her. I listened again for voices or footsteps but there was only the tomb-like silence of Helldon. Most old buildings creaked and sighed, but Helldon was a building that held its breath.

We made our way to the open front door. We were nearly there — we were nearly free — but my stomach was leaden with fear. This would not be a swift escape as it had been with Piglet. I had been terribly frightened at the Hardys' house, but, looking back now, rescuing Piglet seemed such an easy thing to do . . . I could not carry Mama in my arms. We would have to go at her pace. And she was much, much weaker than I had thought.

'We're going to walk a little further, Mama,' I said. 'Do you think you can walk a little further?' She nodded and I thought I saw something in her face – the tiniest glimpse of my old Mama – clever, determined.

We were outside the building now. The sky had darkened further and a cool drizzle dampened the air. We started walking towards the tree-lined driveway. The old grey serpent curled away in front of us. *Thisss way*, it hissed. *Thisss way* . . . But I had another plan. We would cut across the grass. It would be quicker, and the grass would be kinder to Mama's bare feet. We had just made it to the shelter of the first tree when a voice called out loudly behind us, cutting through the wet air like a knife. I froze.

'Miss Abbott,' the voice called. It was not an angry or aggressive voice, it was perfectly calm, and that made it all the more terrifying. I looked around.

A man was walking across the grass towards us. He was short, handsome and dark-haired and was wearing an expensive-looking suit. He looked like an actor in a moving picture. His hands were in his pockets and he was walking quite casually, as if he were simply taking a stroll around the grounds.

'Taking your mother for a bit of fresh air, I see?'

I swallowed painfully and nodded. I turned away from him and urged Mama to take a few more pitifully slow steps. The drizzle gave way to heavier, steadier rain. Mama's feet were getting wet and muddy. 'Just keep walking, Mama,' I breathed. 'Just keep walking.' The route back to the main gate was a long sweep of rain-drenched grass and trees. Walking so slowly, against the slope, against the rain, it would take us fifteen minutes at least . . . With no effort at all, the man was soon strolling along beside us.

'So you're Henrietta,' he said.

I didn't say anything. My eyes were fixed on the gate – a black smudge beyond the heavy curtain of rain. Mama was leaning on my shoulder now, I could feel her losing strength with each step.

'I'm Doctor Chilvers, perhaps you've heard of me . . .'

I blinked with confusion, but kept walking. *Chilvers?* My thoughts scrambled like pieces on an overturned chess board. *But if he is Doctor Chilvers, who on earth is the limping man – the man who has been creeping around Hope House?* I couldn't make sense of any of it. The only thing I knew was that if this was Chilvers, Mama and I had to get away from him.

'Doctor Hardy has told me all about you, Henrietta, and I've been most eager to meet you. He says you claim to be friends with a dead woman called Mrs Young – is that right? And you wander about in the garden, talking to the ghost of your dead brother? I should love you to tell me about these visions of yours, Henrietta. I could help, you know — I could make it all go away . . .'

41

I shook my head and angry tears ran down my cheeks, lost amongst the raindrops. I was panting for breath now – from despair, and from the effort of keeping Mama upright and moving forwards. Another voice boomed behind us. Doctor Hardy.

'There you are!' His voice was thick with rage. I didn't look back – I didn't need to. I pictured his heavy frame lumbering across the grass towards us. 'What the *hell* do you think you're doing, Henrietta?'

'Now, now, Hardy,' said Doctor Chilvers. 'We're just having a little walk together, nothing to be worried about.' He used words in the same way that a surgeon uses a scalpel – deft, confident.

I heard Hardy wheezing. I felt the tremor of his heavy footsteps. 'Just having a little walk?' he gasped furiously. Then he snorted with laughter. 'Ha! I see. Excellent, Chilvers, excellent!'

I was still urging Mama to keep moving. It was hopeless, I knew, but what else could I do? The rain was pouring down now – it battered the grass, pounding it into a grey swamp. The green nightdress clung to Mama like seaweed. We were drowning together. Mama's foot slid in the wet grass and her ankle turned beneath her. She gasped and I caught her as she staggered.

Then Hardy wheeled in front of us – a vast, dripping megalith. 'Where exactly do you think you're going?' he spat scornfully. 'Do you think you are helping your mother by doing this, Henrietta? She needs to be here, for God's sake! We are doctors! We will make her better.'

Even then, knowing all I did about Chilvers' experiments and Hardy's ambition, the obedient child within me wanted to give in. I wanted so much to trust these grown-ups, but I knew that I couldn't. My heart told me that if I left my mother here, she would never come home.

Chilvers tried a different strategy. 'This weather's taken a turn for the worse, hasn't it, Miss Abbott?' He chuckled, blinking up into the rain and the glowering skies above. He took his hand from his pocket and placed it warmly upon my shoulder, steering us back towards the drive. 'Why don't we all step inside and have a nice cup of tea and a chat? Let's get your mother into some dry clothes, shall we?' He was cleverer than Hardy, I had to give him that. He was much cleverer.

If I attempted to struggle on, I knew that they would force me back into Helldon whether I wanted to go or not. They would lock Mama back in her room – she would be a prisoner again and I would be their prisoner too . . . My mind spun around like a cornered rat.

Chilvers offered Mama a gentlemanly arm. She took it and, just for a second, the doctor's kindly mask dropped away. Something like greed glittered in his eyes.

'No!' I shouted, pulling Mama back towards me. Chilvers smiled dangerously. Then several things happened all at once. Hardy lurched towards me, and I backed away. My heel caught on the edge of the driveway and I stumbled, falling backwards. There was a whirring and clattering and a shrill, frightened whinnying. I twisted around in terror. Four sharp hooves danced on the road and the huge wheels of a cart were spinning towards me. Mama screamed.

Then Mr Berry was there, bending down towards me, his face white with shock, but someone else was with him – I squinted dizzily through the downpour – there was a woman too. She stood a few yards away, blurred behind a veil of rain.

'Are you all right, Miss?' Mr Berry said, helping me

to my feet. He was ignoring the doctors completely. 'I saw you standing at the gates and . . . well, I decided to come back and see if you needed any help. *I'll be b-blowed if I'm letting that little 'un go into Helldon all by herself*, I said to myself.' And he wrapped a blanket around me. 'Met your Aunt Susan on the Hawkham Road – seems she was on her way here too.'

I stared at him. *Aunt Susan?* But I didn't actually *have* an Aunt Susan – that had been a lie to bully the Hardys into giving Piglet back . . .

The mysterious figure walked through the rain towards me. She was dressed in a long dark coat. It was only when she was right in front of me that I could see her face. *Moth!* Her wild hair was swept up beneath a broad-brimmed hat. Her eyes shone like steel.

'Let's take you and your mother back home, shall we, Henrietta?' she said, helping us both up into the carriage. Mr Berry took another blanket from the back of the trap and wrapped it around Mama's shivering shoulders.

The two doctors had been silent all this time, watching the whole pantomime with folded arms. Chilvers finally stepped forward, smoothing his wet hair down with a neat paw. 'Good Lord,' he said, squinting into the rain. 'Is that Sergeant Berry? Never thought we'd see you again, S-Sergeant. I see you made it through the rest of the war, then . . . How's the st-st-stutter, eh?' He and Doctor Hardy chuckled.

Mr Berry took a deep breath. He turned to face Chilvers. As he spoke, his eyes twitched, but his voice was as steady as a rock.

'I'll be taking Miss Abbott and her mother home now, Doctor Chilvers,' he said.

We all squeezed into the trap together.

'You can't just go, I'm afraid,' snapped Doctor Hardy. 'There are papers that need to be signed in order to discharge Mrs Abbott. She is legally under our—'

'I'm sure my father will be happy to discuss everything with you when he returns,' I managed to say.

Chilvers laughed out loud.

'When he *returns*?' Hardy guffawed. 'You think he's coming back? I've seen a fair few cases like this over the years, Miss Abbott – happens all the time – some people just can't cope – they run away from their problems. Your father has gone. If he ever comes home, I'll eat my hat . . .'

Moth spoke now. Her voice was stone cold. 'I'm sure my brother will be home very soon,' she said. 'Just as Henrietta says. And I shall return shortly to sign the necessary papers – I will be bringing along the royal nerve specialist I mentioned on the telephone earlier. Shouldn't be more than a few hours.' I noticed Moth angled her head very carefully as she spoke, so that the brim of her hat covered as much of her face as possible.

Doctor Hardy was purple with rage. As he looked at

Moth, though, his face started to change. 'Have we met before, Madam?' he said. And then took a step towards us. 'I think, perhaps—'

'There are those,' Moth said to Hardy, her voice louder now, 'who believe your methods are medieval, Doctor Hardy. You are blinded by ignorance and ambition. You see only symptoms. You do not see people, and you do not see the damage you do to them.'

'Poppycock!' exclaimed Chilvers. He laughed but he was trembling with anger. Doctor Hardy was staring at Moth now. He must have recognized her . . . She tilted her head up a little and looked straight back at him. Her eyes glared, cold and metallic, but I saw that her lips were bloodless and were pressed tightly together. She was frightened.

'Let's go, Mr Berry,' I hissed. 'Quickly!' And, with shaking hands, he turned the pony around.

The doctors stood side by side, underneath a tree dripping with rain – a purple giant and a white dwarf – like a comical drawing from a newspaper.

'Mrs Abbott has been committed to this asylum,' Doctor Hardy shouted impotently. 'She is insane! I don't know what exactly this ridiculous charade is supposed to achieve.' He pointed at Moth: 'And if you're Henrietta's Aunt Susan, I'm a monkey's uncle!'

'If the cap fits, Doctor Hardy,' I called back to him from the safety of the carriage, and I saw then that there was fear and confusion in his eyes as well as rage.

He had been present at the inquest, he had witnessed the signing of the death certificate for Mrs Young – and now here she was, right in front of him, as large as life!

'Such a pleasure to see you again,' Moth called, removing her hat triumphantly and turning to wave at the doctors. 'Goodbye!'

'Trot on, Bert,' called Mr Berry. The brown pony was moving quickly now. Moth's arm was around my shoulders. We were following the snaking driveway back towards the tall iron gates, and Helldon was behind us.

42

I lay on Mama's bed, facing her, my back to the
window, our foreheads almost touching, our
knees drawn up together. From above we might
have looked like the white wings of a butterfly. I spent
the first few hours of the night wide awake, holding
her hand, talking to her softly. The rain continued to
fall, steadily, heavily. The sky flashed a few times and I
heard the low rumble of distant thunder.

It must have been past midnight when I heard the
creak of a floorboard on the landing, and the door to
Mama's room swung open. I turned to see a figure
standing in the doorway, a figure wrapped once more
in her familiar blankets and holding a key in her hand.
Moth.

'I'm sorry – I didn't mean to frighten you,' she

whispered. 'I had to come and see . . .' She walked towards the bed. 'How is she?' She gazed down at Mama, and stroked the hair from her forehead, checking her temperature.

Mama's eyes opened then. 'Oh!' she said, smiling sleepily. 'Oh, I thought, perhaps, I had dreamt you . . .' and her face became as radiant as a child's. 'My nightingale . . .'

There was a noise from further down the landing. A distressed cry, a door opening and closing, soft murmurs . . . Piglet was awake and Nanny Jane had gone to her. Perhaps she was having a bad dream about the Hardys, or perhaps it was just the thunder.

Something changed in Mama's face. It was an expression I hadn't seen before – a longing. Her eyes filled with tears. Moth smiled gently and took her hand. 'Come with me,' she whispered. She led her from the bedroom to the secret attic door. I took the candle from Mama's bedside table and followed close behind. What an odd procession we must have made – Moth in her ragged blankets at the front, and Mama and I in our ghost-white nightdresses, climbing those dusty stairs by candlelight. I noticed how Moth's feet trod the most worn patches of carpet: she had walked these steps many times before.

Moth stood at the cartwheel window and gazed out towards the sea. She looked such a natural part of this attic room, this fairy-tale turret – a moth amongst ancient cobwebs.

I turned around and looked at Mama. She was sitting on the bed, looking pale and confused.

'I've been here before,' she said. Her eyes were dark and huge. 'I thought – I dreamt it was Robert's room.'

'Not Robert's room, Mama,' I said gently. 'Alfred's.'

She looked around the room slowly, and noticed the model ships on the shelf.

'Alfred . . .' she echoed. 'He likes ships, like Robert used to. Where is little Alfred?'

Moth came to sit beside Mama. She pulled the photograph from a pocket beneath her blanket.

'Oh,' Mama said, touching the picture. 'What a lovely little chap . . . Alfred . . .'

Mama looked at Moth, then looked back at the photograph. I saw that she was studying the face of the young nurse and the child.

'Your boy?' she asked – her voice was barely audible.

'My boy,' Moth said, hoarsely. 'He – died in the war.'

Mama gazed sadly at the photograph, then turned it over. 'He wrote this – on the back – *1907, me and Moth*?'

Moth shook her head, her eyes sparkling. 'Freddie wrote it, yes, but . . . it doesn't say Moth . . .' She couldn't continue.

It doesn't say Moth? I looked at the back of the

photograph now and for the first time I understood the mistake I had made.

Moth was not called Moth and she never had been. The photograph was torn at the corner, and two letters were missing. Years ago, little Alfred had written: *1907, me and Mother*.

Moth put the photograph safely back in her pocket. The two women looked into each other's eyes and something silent was said between them, something I didn't understand. Moth stretched her arms around Mama, enveloping her in a warm blanket. Mama folded in half, shaking.

Moth spoke to her. Pity thickened her voice. 'There is hope,' she said. 'There is so much hope. Just look at this one. She shines like a star . . .'

Was she talking about me?

'She always has.' Mama tried to smile through her tears. 'But I can't – the doctors said I couldn't look after them . . .' And her face crumpled with grief. 'Robert died and then they took my girls away from me too. They said I wasn't fit to look after them – I never even held the baby . . .'

Piglet. *She has never even held Piglet*. All this time, Mama had thought it was somehow her fault that the baby had been taken from her . . . I thought about the tears rolling down her face as I read Rumpelstiltskin.

'No,' Moth said. 'She is yours. The doctors were

wrong. The baby is yours and so is this one. They need their mother now. It's not too late for you. It's not too late . . .' Moth was stroking Mama's back in the same way that I stroked Piglet when she cried.

'I don't know how to get back,' Mama gasped, and her voice was ragged with fear.

'You can,' Moth said through her tears. 'You can. You will.' And her words were carved in stone.

43

Mrs Berry came to work as usual the next day. When I went into the kitchen she put her arms around me and said Mr Berry sent his very best wishes to both me and Mama. 'Thank you,' I muttered into her shoulder. 'Please tell him thank you.' I couldn't say anything else so I just squeezed Mrs Berry's floury hands and then helped her to knead some dough.

'Archie said you had some help yesterday,' Mrs Berry said quietly as we worked. 'Said he couldn't believe his eyes when he saw her walking along the Hawkham Road in the rain – just like a ghost lady, he said.'

I didn't say anything. So Mr Berry had known that she wasn't really my aunt – he had recognized her as

Mrs Young. I smiled at his kindness in playing along.

'Where's she been all these years?' Mrs Berry asked. 'The poor lost soul . . .'

I looked through the kitchen door towards Nightingale Wood. What could I say? 'Not lost, Mrs Berry,' I said. 'She just didn't want to be found.'

It was a quiet day, still and overcast, as if nature were recovering from the storm. Mama slept a great deal, but it seemed to be a different sort of sleep now that she was no longer drugged – peaceful, healing. I sat on the bed and read to her as she slept. I read *The Nightingale* because it was her favourite story, and because it reminded me of Moth.

Nanny Jane slept for much of the day too. She was almost as exhausted as Mama, I think. Although our situation at Hope House appeared to be just as it was a week or so ago, before Piglet and Mama were both taken away, I knew that was not actually the case. Something important had changed. It was as if we had all been broken, and then put back together in a slightly different way. A better way, I thought – stronger than we had been before.

Piglet was unusually grumpy that afternoon. She had started to shake her head to say 'No' – frowning and grunting crossly, 'Mm!' at the same time – a trick she had learnt at the Hardys, perhaps. She must have done this a hundred times between lunch and tea time. She shook her head at her bottle of milk, at the sweet mush of carrots and roast chicken Mrs Berry made for her — at everything she was offered. When I tried singing nursery rhymes to her she shook her head so angrily that the effect was almost comical: 'Humpty Dumpty' made her particularly cross.

In just a few days she would be one year old. I wondered if her birthday would pass like mine, forgotten. I hadn't mentioned it and no one else had either. I decided I wouldn't let that happen to Piglet and, just before her bath time, I took her back into the kitchen to see Mrs Berry and plan a birthday tea party for the following week. Mrs Berry was delighted and sat down straight away to make a shopping list.

We were well past midsummer now. The sky would have been deep blue at this hour a month ago; now it was pale and silvery. The kitchen door and windows were open wide and a blackbird was singing his heart out in the apple tree near the roses. Mrs Berry would be off home soon. While she tidied the kitchen and finished the shopping list for Piglet's tea party, I stood by the back door, bouncing Piglet gently in my arms. She nuzzled into my neck, squirming unhappily. *She must be very tired*, I thought. I kept talking to her in a low voice, patting her back. I told her about the birds in the garden — a blackbird, a robin, and a round little wren who darted amongst the leaves like a field mouse with wings.

Piglet became heavier in my arms now, snuffling sleepily. She dribbled on my shoulder. I kept patting her. 'Listen Piglet,' I whispered. 'What can you hear? Mrs Berry splashing at the sink, the church bells chiming, the blackbird's evening song, a motor car on the road from the village . . .'

I took Piglet up to the nursery and put her straight down in her cot. It didn't seem like a good idea to wake her for a bath. She grunted, rolled on to her side and fell instantly and deeply asleep.

Nanny Jane was still resting in her bedroom and Mrs Berry had gone home for the day. The house was quiet. I went into Mama's room and I sat down on the end of her bed. The windows were open. The air was soft and heavy with the silence of the evening. She was smiling in her sleep.

I was suddenly aware of a noise outside the front of the house. The churning of a motor car engine, the slowing crunch of tyres on gravel. That sound had come to mean one thing to me: Doctor Hardy.

He is back. I thought. *He is back to take Mama to Helldon again, to lock me up too; to put us both in straitjackets . . .* I was hot and cold at once. My palms were moist and I could feel my heart beating in my throat, in every fingertip. Doctor Hardy was a ghoul at the desk behind me, calmly completing the paperwork to have me locked away . . . A car door opened and closed. Foot-steps came towards the house. I looked at the white curtains fluttering at the window but was too afraid to part them and look outside. I didn't think I could even stand up – it felt as if my legs were drained of blood.

I heard a key turning in the lock of the front door. *A key?* My heart understood the sound before I did and it leapt in my chest. I gasped and flew to the window, both hands pressed to the glass as I looked down, open-mouthed, into the driveway. It wasn't Doctor Hardy's motor car standing in front of the house; it was a different car altogether – *Oh!* It was a car I had not seen for a long time.

Father had never been one for affectionate embraces but on this occasion I'm afraid I gave him very little choice. I flew down the stairs and flung myself into him, sobbing with relief to feel his arms around me. He smelt of summer air and engines and pipe smoke and faraway places. I pressed my face to his chest and breathed him in with each sob. He just held me and kissed the top of my head. 'I'm home now, Hen. I'm home now,' he said.

'You're home,' I sobbed. 'I knew you'd come. Doctor Hardy will have to eat his hat!'

He held me away from him and looked at me with a confused smile. 'He'll have to what?' Then he hugged me again. 'It was your telegram, Hen,' he said. 'The telegram you sent yesterday morning.'

I thought of the words I had chosen. I had only had enough money for four of them. It was agonizing – how could I possibly explain everything that was happening in just four words? In the end, the words I chose were these:

We need you here.

44

'It's not like Helldon at all, Hen,' Father said. 'It's a very special sort of hospital.'

We were eating supper in the kitchen together. Father had opened a can of pea and ham soup and warmed it up in a pan on the stove. I had cut some thick slices of Mrs Berry's homemade bread and spread them with butter. We ate by the yellow light of the oil lamp instead of the bright gaslights of the dining room. Although we were in our own kitchen, it felt as if we were on an adventure, camping out together in a strange new wilderness.

'A special sort of hospital?' I wondered if he could hear the dismay in my voice.

'Yes,' Father said. 'Your mother will be well looked after properly, I promise.'

I thought about the night after I brought Mama home. While I had lain next to Mama, holding both her hands in mine, Father had suffered a sleepless, stormy night. He had spent the whole of that day travelling back from Italy to France and had crossed the English Channel overnight in a storm, the sea bucking and churning beneath a thunderous sky: the same thunder that we had heard in the distance, that had awoken little Piglet. Father had caught the first train to London, had collected his car and driven straight back to Hope House.

He looked tired, but not in the same way that he had before he left us all those weeks before. There was something new in his eyes — something a little brighter. I thought, perhaps, that it might be hope.

Father's spoon scraped the last of the soup from his bowl. He stood up and took our crockery over to the sink. With his back to the lamp, his face was hidden in shadow.

'I met a doctor in the Alps — Wolfgang Berger — an Austrian gentleman who was staying at my hotel. A kind man, and a wise one too. We talked in the evenings. I told him about . . . everything that has happened. Herr Berger is a sort of nerve doctor, Hen. He has been working at a hospital in Switzerland. When I met him, he was just about to leave Italy, to start work at a new clinic in London. I told him about Doctor Hardy and Doctor Chilvers and Helldon. He had some interesting things to say . . .'

I got up from the table, found a tea towel, and started drying the plates, bowls and cutlery Father was washing. I stacked them on the table. It was almost dark outside. I was aware that, the darker it became, the more quietly we were talking. I knew that, in the morning, this strange, lamp-lit conversation would feel like a dream.

'When I got your telegram, I told my employer I had to return home urgently. Doctor Berger and I travelled to Paris together to catch the boat train. I'm going to take Mama to his hospital in London, Hen.'

I must have looked upset. *Another hospital. Another doctor. Why can't Mama just stay at home?*

'It's a good place, Henry,' he said firmly. 'A different sort of place. Not all doctors are like Hardy or Chilvers. They will look after her, I promise. They will be very gentle. They will talk to her and give her the right sort of medicine and help her to get better.'

I interrupted him. 'They aren't going to give her a tropical disease?'

He stopped washing up and looked straight at me. 'No, Henry,' he said.

'Or put her in freezing water, or do an operation on her?'

'No. No, they won't.' He pressed his lips together, swallowed hard and ran a dish mop around the inside of the pan he had used to warm the soup.

'But Doctor Hardy said . . .'

Father shook his head. It was identical to Piglet's stubborn little gesture; it was an unequivocal 'no'. 'I have spoken to Doctor Hardy,' he said, 'and his colleague at the asylum. I have made my feelings about their treatments very clear.'

And something that had sat heavily in my heart all that summer – a knot, a rock, a jagged chunk of ice – started to melt away. I knew then that Doctor Hardy and his orders would not be returning to Hope House.

After a moment Father said, 'It was very brave of you, Hen, to go to Helldon all by yourself and bring Mama home. To get Piglet back too. And I'm – I'm so sorry that I wasn't here when you needed me most. I should never have gone away when I did.'

'That's all right,' I murmured, looking at the floor. I had never heard Father say he had been wrong about anything.

He held my chin in his soapy hand for a moment and looked at me. His eyes shone strangely. Then he picked up his dish mop again.

When we had finished tidying up, Father opened the kitchen door and sat outside on the step. I sat down next to him. He took his pipe from his pocket, stuffed it with fragrant tobacco, and lit a match. The pipe glowed warmly – a circle of orange light. Pipe smoke curled up into the evening air, smelling of cherries and leather and spiced wine. We sat quietly together. I gazed up at the sky, watching the first stars emerge from the deepening darkness. I was reminded of that first night at Hope House, when I had looked out of the kitchen door and the garden had been an underwater world.

'I tried to write to you,' I said. 'But I couldn't find the right words. I ended up writing a story about a moth and a nightingale, and an Impossible Mountain . . .' I looked at the ground, waiting for Father to tell me that I was too old for fairy tales.

He paused. 'I should like to read that,' he said. 'I should like to read that very much, Hen.'

I felt something warm and happy blossoming in my chest.

Then he said, 'Mama said something about a nightingale – when I was talking to her before supper. Someone who has been looking after her, perhaps? Someone who helped you yesterday? I'm sure she called her a nightingale . . .'

I nodded.

'I couldn't work out if she meant a real person or – something else. Your Mama was smiling, Hen,' he said. 'I haven't seen her smile like that since before——' His voice cracked. I froze. Would he be able to say it?

'Since before your brother died,' he said finally, and drew on his pipe.

We were sitting so close to each other. I wanted to lean over and kiss his tired cheek, but I didn't.

'Do you know who she was talking about?' he asked. 'The nightingale?'

'Yes,' I said. 'Yes, I do.'

He nodded and waited for me to explain. When I didn't say anything more, he just looked at me and smiled. I smiled back. I think it was the loveliest moment we'd ever shared.

He didn't need me to tell him about Mama and the nightingale. It was enough that I understood.

45

I slept and slept that night. I slept like a hibernating creature curled up in its safe, dark den. When I awoke, the sun was already high in the sky and I could hear the low buzz of male voices in conversation downstairs.

I found a clean pinafore, dressed quickly and padded down the stairs, barefoot. The hall was empty. Nanny Jane was in the dining room with Piglet. She waved to me as I passed the door. She looked better than she had in weeks, her hair was brushed neatly back into her usual tight blonde bun, her cheeks were scrubbed pink and white.

'Shall I ask Mrs Berry to make some fresh porridge, Henry?' she called after me.

'Yes, please,' I called back. 'In a minute . . .'

I walked back along the corridor and through the hallway, my feet making no sound. The voices buzzed once more. I followed them to the doorway of Father's study and peered inside.

'Please forgive the mess,' Father was saying from behind his desk. 'I haven't really had a chance to finish unpacking yet.'

Then the long-legged figure of Mr Pickersgill came into view. He lowered himself down into the armchair by the fireplace. 'Not at all!' he said, twinkling happily as he looked around at the piles of books all over the floor. 'Indeed, it's the system I favour myself.'

I slipped quietly into the room, bidding Father good morning, shaking Mr Pickersgill's hand politely and taking a seat next to the window.

The two men talked about Europe and Italy and the project Father had been working on – the Simplon Tunnel through the Alps. They talked about the Treaty of Versailles and the unrest in Germany – protests, violence, uprisings. Peace was not, apparently, simply the absence of war – it was more complicated than that. At last, with resigned shakes of the head, the pace of the conversation slowed.

'It's nice to see you again, Mr Pickersgill. We didn't really get a chance to say goodbye properly last time,' I said, thinking of our strange conversation in the archives of Solomon and Pickersgill, and my sudden exit.

Father raised his eyebrows quizzically.

'Yes,' Mr Pickersgill replied, with a smile. 'I do apologize, Miss Abbott.' He turned towards Father. 'Your daughter came to tell me something and I was rather blunt, I'm afraid. It was – shocking news, you see, and I was convinced that she was wrong . . . But it turns out that she was right.' He looked back at me and smiled again. 'Mrs Berry came to see me first thing this morning. This news is – not unrelated to the reason for my visit, as a matter of fact.'

I held my breath. Was he going to tell Father everything? That I had befriended a person believed to be dead . . . That the late Mrs Young was actually alive – and living in our woods?

'I wanted to talk to you about your requested extension of the tenancy contract, Mr Abbott. I feel obliged to warn you that there is a possibility that Hope House may not be available for rent in the future.'

Father frowned.

'The legal owner has recently . . . come to light, shall we say, and it is not impossible that, in time, she may choose to live here once more.'

Moth, he was talking about Moth. How wonderful it would be for her to return to Hope House – but how terrible if we had to leave . . .

'I thought you said the house was owned by people in Ireland,' Father said.

'Yes. Well, it *was* until — I mean, technically it still is . . . Oh dear, I'm afraid it's rather complicated. The legal owner was thought to be dead, you see. She disappeared in 1916, after her son was killed in the war, but it seems . . .' He shrugged, and his smile was helpless but undeniably happy. 'It seems that she is alive after all.'

'She disappeared after her son's death?' Father's words were quite haunting. Perhaps he was thinking of Mama.

'Yes. She always said that he was her whole world. He was her son.'

Father nodded, confused. The point seemed obvious.

'No — her *sun*,' Mr Pickersgill repeated. He gestured to the summer sky outside the window.

Father's jaw tightened and, with a flutter of dismay, I saw that he was trying not to cry.

Quickly, and with an air of apology, Mr Pickersgill chose this moment to reread one of the documents he had brought with him. He muttered about the complexities of property law, all the while keeping his eyes glued to the paper. Father stared at the window, breathing and blinking.

I allowed myself to be soothed by the sound of Mr Pickersgill's voice, and my thoughts turned to Mama. Father was going to take her to Doctor Berger's hospital in London that afternoon. I tried to erase the images of Helldon that haunted my mind: locked doors, barred windows, dark corridors. I tried to paint over these horrors with what Father had told me about his friend's new clinic in Bloomsbury: open windows, books, gentle voices . . .

After a minute, and with a quick glance at Father, Mr Pickersgill brought his rambling to an end. He shuffled his papers, stood up, and smiled warmly at us both. He twinkled kindly and said, 'The owner's wishes are not known at present, Mr Abbott, but I will keep you informed about any developments. The house is, of course, yours until the end of October, as per the original tenancy agreement. If it transpires that you need to find another property in the area after that, I shall do everything I possibly can to help you and your family.'

Father thanked him. I saw how grateful he was for Mr Pickersgill's tact and kindness. I saw that they might, perhaps, become good friends.

'And now,' started Mr Pickersgill, 'I need to talk to your daughter concerning . . . a mutual friend of ours. Shall we take a turn around the garden, Miss Abbott?'

Father smiled a pleasantly confused smile, and looked at me with surprise and pride. He shook Mr Pickersgill's hand, turned back to his desk, and started opening a pile of letters.

46

'So, you believe me now?' I said as we stepped through the kitchen door and out on to the terrace. 'You believe that Moth is Mrs Young?' It was a bright morning, with a fresh breeze. A flotilla of white clouds sailed across the broad blue sky. We walked side by side down the length of the lawn.

'Yes, I do,' Mr Pickersgill conceded, keeping his eyes on his shoes. Then he smiled drily. 'Mrs Berry told me all about your mysterious Aunt Susan.'

I blushed. I tried to keep step with him as we headed towards the pond. The lawn felt deliciously cool beneath my bare feet. I scrunched my toes through the dew-damp grass. We sat down on the moss-covered bench.

'I wasn't just the family solicitor, you know. I

tutored her boy, Alfred,' Mr Pickersgill said. 'Did I tell you that before, when you——? No, perhaps I didn't.'

'No, you didn't tell me,' I said.

'Freddie was an ambitious boy – when he was about twelve he decided that he wanted to become an admiral in the Navy. His mother asked me to help him with his school work in the holidays. After I had taught Freddie, Niamh and I would sit together in the library and talk – about books usually . . . We became very good friends.'

'Niamh?' I had never heard the name before.

'Niamh.' He said it again so I could pronounce it properly: 'Nee-uhv.' It was a strange and lovely word. *Niamh. Not Moth. Niamh Young.*

'It's an Irish name,' Mr Pickersgill said. 'It means bright. Radiant.'

It was perfect for her.

Mr Pickersgill shook his head, but he kept talking. Perhaps he felt the same compulsion I did: the same desire for things to finally make sense – to connect.

'We became close. A bit like a family really. The family I never had. But when I returned from the war last winter, they were both gone. Both of them.'

Mr Pickersgill was grasping a brown envelope in his hands and it was becoming crushed and dog-eared as he spoke. I took it from him, gently, and smoothed the corners.

He drew in a long, deep breath.

'In the space of just a few years – while I was stuck in that hell – Freddie grew up and went to war, and Niamh vanished from the face of the earth.'

'When Mrs Young disappeared,' I said, 'she left a note?'

Mr Pickersgill nodded. 'It said she couldn't go on and asked me to look after Hope House. After the coroner's verdict the house was passed to her family – distant cousins in Ireland – but I took care of all the administration and maintenance. They wanted to sell it, but I persuaded them not to. Ridiculous really . . . Part of me refused to believe she had gone. Hope is a funny thing, Miss Abbott. If you cling on to it for too long, it can become something cruel.'

'But you were right,' I said. 'You were right to hope.'

'To think that all that time . . .' He shook his head, slowly. 'She was so near . . . If I'd only known . . .'

We were both quiet for a while, our eyes moving from the murky pond to the colourful chaos of the flower beds, the ruins of the gazebo, and finally to Hope House itself, shambolic and beautiful, leaning slightly towards us, as if it were a friendly eavesdropper.

'Freddie was the closest thing to a son I ever had,' Mr Pickersgill said, with a smile. 'And – well, with his father having died so young, he became very attached to me too. He used to call me Oncle Fidèle.'

'*Fidèle*? That means faithful, doesn't it? Loyal?'

'Oncle Fidèle was a little joke of Freddie's. Just a little joke, but it stuck somehow. Fidèle was his school-boy-French translation of my Christian name.'

Truman Pickersgill. True man. I smiled. Freddie and Robert would have got along very well together.

Mr Pickersgill had taken the envelope back from me and was staring at it now. He seemed nervous. There was something he wasn't telling me.

'I was hoping you would take me to see her, Henri-etta,' he said. 'There is a great deal of paperwork to do with the Hope House estate,' he said. Then he looked me in the eye. 'And there is something else too . . .'

As we entered the woods, I saw that the spindle tree at the edge of the forest was already starting to ripen its bright red fruit, and I wondered how long it would be before the whole tree was ablaze with autumn colour. Not long, perhaps. The summer was almost over.

It was cool beneath the shade of the trees, and quiet, too. I pulled my cardigan tightly around myself, step-ping carefully on the path with my bare feet. A breeze pushed and pulled at the leaves of the outermost trees so that they said, 'Shhhh, shhhh,' and everything beyond them obeyed. The birds were silent. Nothing could be heard apart from the tread of our four rather mismatched feet. I realized that I had not hesitated even for a moment before entering the darkness of the woods. It seemed that I was not the slightest bit afraid any more.

Mr Pickersgill, on the other hand, was behaving very strangely. He kept checking his watch and looking over his shoulder, as if to see if someone was following us. What had he meant by 'there is something else too'? He had refused to explain.

'Is everything all right, Mr Pickersgill?' I said.

'Yes. Quite all right,' he said, clearing his throat nervously. 'This is just – a little odd. I don't know what I shall say to her.'

'I'm sure you will know when you see her,' I said. 'You were good friends, after all. She's still the same person.'

'But how could she possibly be the same person?' he asked, looking all around. 'Imagine three years on your own . . . Three winters in this forest . . . It would change you into a different creature entirely.'

I understood. But for me it was the other way around: it was Moth I knew; Niamh Young was the unknowable creature.

'Have you changed that much?' I asked, carefully pinching a stray bramble and moving it from our path.

'War changes people,' he said, after a moment. 'War and loneliness . . .' I looked back at him and saw the corners of his mouth lift a little. 'But, now that you mention it, Miss Abbott, I do believe that, somewhere deep down inside, I feel exactly as I did when I was your age. Perhaps there is a part of us that always remains true.'

47

Moth was sitting beside her fire, singing to herself and darning holes in a particularly threadbare blanket.

'Your father is home, Henrietta,' she said.

'Yes,' I said. 'He is.' And I felt a wave of joy surge through me at the thought of his return.

'And your mother?'

'Getting stronger,' I said.

She smiled her crooked smile and held her hands out to me. Then she noticed that I wasn't alone.

Mr Pickersgill walked into the centre of the clearing and stood quite still, waiting. Moth didn't say anything at all, and neither did I. I sat down beside the fire. Mr Pickersgill shuffled awkwardly, then he folded his long legs and sat down next to me. His trousers rode up to reveal a pair of bony shins clad in brightly patterned socks. I saw that he was shaking, and he clasped his knees tightly. Moth's eyes followed his every movement.

We were all silent.

Somewhere in the depths of the forest, a woodpecker drilled at a hollow tree.

Mr Pickersgill looked at the papers, and they quivered in his hand. He nodded and cleared his throat. When he spoke, his voice was so quiet I could barely hear it over the popping of the fire.

'Hello, Niamh,' he said.

'Hello, Truman,' Moth replied softly.

'When Miss Abbott told me she thought Mrs Young was living here, in the woods, I said, No, Mrs Young died three ago. She is dead. Her name is on a gravestone. I put flowers . . .' His voice broke and he stopped. He looked into Moth's eyes for the first time.

My heart tightened and I held my breath.

'I put *flowers* . . .' he said again, hoarsely.

'I'm sorry,' Moth said. 'I'm so sorry, Truman. After Freddie – I just couldn't . . .'

They stared at each other for a moment, heartbreak brimming in their eyes.

'I know,' Mr Pickersgill said at last. 'I understand.' He leant forward and passed her the envelope, taking her hand for a moment. 'There is money that is yours,

Niamh,' he said. 'A house that is yours. You can come home now.'

She shook her head. 'That house is no good to me.'

'You can't spend another winter alone in the woods,' I said. 'Mr Pickersgill just wants to—'

· 'My answer is no, Henrietta. It's hard here in winter, very hard, but – how could I just go back? I've been dead for three years – I can't go back.'

I didn't understand what she meant. She had been so brave. She had left the woods and walked to Helldon. She had confronted Doctor Hardy . . .

'It was different at Helldon,' she said, reading my mind. 'I was playing a part. To help you, Henrietta. It wasn't real life, was it? That's the difference. And when Hardy recognized me, I . . .' She took a deep breath. 'I can't do it. I can't just go back to being Mrs Young of Hope House, paying the butcher's bill and chatting with the postman as if nothing ever happened. I don't know how to be that person any more. I've been free. I've been part of the forest . . .'

'But—'

'Hope House is my past, Henrietta. My last memories of that place are terrible – lonely, haunted . . . But your family have a future there. You can be happy – you and your parents and your little sister.'

'Please, Niamh,' Mr Pickersgill said. 'Just think about it.'

Moth sighed, and then opened the brown envelope.

It was a wad of paper: copies of property deeds, lists of accounts, statements from a bank.

'I will take care of everything,' Mr Pickersgill said quietly, trying not to make her angry. 'I promise to be discreet . . . No fuss or fanfare.'

Moth shuffled through the papers, shaking her head.

'This all belongs to me?' she said, and I thought that something was softening.

'Yes – all of it.'

'Then it is mine to do with as I please.'

Mr Pickersgill looked flustered.

Moth just shook her head, smiled her crooked smile and said firmly, 'I'm not going back there, Truman.'

She put the papers down on the ground and went back to her darning.

I looked at the pile of documents. The deeds for Hope House were on the top, but they seemed to be attached to another set of deeds. I picked them up and looked more closely: *Gamekeeper's Cottage, Frith Meadow*.

'You own that old house?' I said. 'At the edge of the forest?' It was the tumbledown cottage I had found on the day I had got so lost.

'It was part of the Hope House estate,' Moth said. 'An old ruin – just like me.' And she smiled again.

'But you could live there,' I said. 'If you wanted to, I mean . . . You would be with the birds and the animals, still part of the forest, still miles away from anybody, but you would be safe and warm. It would be a proper home for you.'

Mr Pickersgill nodded encouragingly. 'A wonderful idea! I could get it all fixed up for you to move into before the winter comes . . .'

Moth looked at the ramshackle caravan, with its rotten roof and dirty, broken windows. Then she nodded very slowly. 'All right, then,' she said at last. 'Thank you.'

Mr Pickersgill took the pile of documents from me, satisfied. 'And there's something else, Niamh,' he said. His voice had changed slightly.

Moth watched him, wary. 'Something else?' Then Moth quickly moved her head and stared into the forest behind me. Her face froze. I heard dead leaves crunching, twigs snapping.

Someone was coming.

There was a thump behind us as Moth's cat leapt up on to the roof of the caravan, his thin body arched with fear. He hissed. He was staring at something I couldn't yet see, something moving towards us through the trees . . .

Then I saw it. A dark shape twisting through the shadows. A stick, a black boot, a dark collar turned up over the jaw of a white face.

It was the limping man.

48

My skin prickled with fear – he had hunted us down – the limping man had found us. I had thought this man was Doctor Chilvers, but I had been wrong. Who *was* he, then? I wanted to run away; I wanted to scream at him to leave us alone. I wanted to throw stones.

Before I had a chance to do anything at all, the limping man came into the clearing. Mr Pickersgill stood up, walked over to him and shook his hand. Then they came towards us and Moth stood up too, slightly crouched, like an animal ready to leap into the undergrowth.

'Mrs Young?' the limping man said.

Moth's mouth twitched, ready to deny it. She hesitated, looked at Mr Pickersgill, then nodded.

I saw the man's face properly for the first time – the predatory, hooded eyes, the missing eyebrows, the skin pulled tightly across his features like a mask. And then I understood. His face was scarred. He had been badly burnt.

'I'm afraid I don't know quite how to begin,' he said. His voice was not the voice of a deranged doctor or a cruel predator at all – it was much more gentle than I was expecting. 'My name is David Stark. Please forgive my intrusion, Mrs Young. I have been looking for you for some time now. But I was told that you were – that you had died.'

'Ah. Yes,' Moth said, somewhat unhelpfully.

David Stark continued: 'Mr Pickersgill contacted me at my hotel—'

'A little hotel by the sea?' I asked, interrupting him. 'With pine trees and sand dunes and blue-green grass?' He nodded, confused.

'I saw you there,' I said, a note of accusation in my voice. 'And I saw you at Hope House too.'

He nodded again but he didn't seem to remember seeing me. I wasn't sure he even saw me now. He turned back to Moth.

'Perhaps we should sit down,' he said. He waited until everyone had settled themselves by the fire again. Then he took a deep breath. 'I'm here because of Freddie, Mrs Young. I served with your son in the Navy.'

Moth's pale face became even paler. 'You . . . knew my Freddie?' she whispered.

'In the Navy, yes,' he said. 'We were very good friends.'

'Friends.' Moth nodded, her mouth open.

'I wanted to find you. I was in a prisoner-of-war camp in Germany, you see, until the end of the war, and I've been in hospital since then . . .' He gestured towards his leg with a half-smile. 'I was in something of a state when they sent me home.'

The limping man was not as I had imagined him to be. There was nothing sinister or frightening about him. He had the most gentlemanly, the most defence-less voice I had ever heard. Silently, I admonished my imagination. I had seen this man's disfigured face, his limping walk, his dark clothes, his stick, and I had turned him into a pantomime villain. I felt ashamed. For the first time, I saw the danger of allowing stories to seep too deeply into reality. Real people simply did not fit the neat black-and-white patterns of fairy tales.

Moth didn't seem to know what to say. 'I'm so sorry to hear that,' she murmured.

Mr Pickersgill was watching them both. 'Mr Stark came to see me at the office, Niamh,' he said gently. 'He was such a good friend of Freddie's, you see. He wanted very much to meet you. At first I sent him away, of course, thinking – as we all did – that you were . . . But then I was able to telephone him this morning with the good news . . .'

'I wanted to find you as soon as I was released from hospital,' David Stark continued. 'You see, Freddie was a hero, Mrs Young.'

Moth's face wore a strange expression I hadn't seen before. It was perfectly still, controlled, but her eyes were like diamonds.

'We trained together,' he went on. 'I was very homesick at first. Like Freddie, I hadn't been away from my family before. We talked, most evenings, about our homes, our families, books . . . We wrote our letters together. He was happy in the Navy. I wanted to tell you that he was happy, Mrs Young, that he spoke of you so warmly and so often.'

Moth could only smile. Her eyes shone. I saw her gulping his words down thirstily. With every word, she was getting back a little more of her boy.

'Did they send you his things from the barracks?' David Stark asked.

'Just his serviceman's bible,' Moth said faintly. 'Just some clothes, his bible and an old photograph.'

'But not this . . .' David Stark pulled a silver pen from his pocket. He gave it to me to pass to Moth. It was a lovely old fountain pen, engraved with the words 'Seaward Ho!'

Moth gasped as I placed it in her hands: 'His pen!'

'It was with my things in the barracks, so it was sent back to my family by mistake. Freddie had lent it to me, the day before we set sail . . .'

'Thank you,' Moth breathed. 'I had it engraved for him when he joined the Navy. It's a quotation—'

'From *Treasure Island*.'

'Yes.' And she gazed at the fountain pen as if it were the most remarkable and beautiful thing she had ever seen. After a moment, and in a quieter voice, Moth said, 'Can you tell me . . .? They told us so little. Do you know how he . . .?'

David Stark couldn't look at her then. He looked instead into the slumbering embers of the fire. 'It was all a terrible blur,' he said. 'After weeks and weeks of nothing happening, the end came so quickly.'

We were quiet.

He continued, in his beautiful voice, 'There weren't many sea battles in the Great War. The Navy didn't lose anywhere near as many men as were lost in the fields of France and Flanders, but still . . . thousands died. Things were quiet for months. Tense and quiet. We were serving on the *HMS Invincible*. We held our line, maintaining a blockade of ships – to prevent supplies getting through to the enemy. Then, one night, we gave chase to a German fleet. They fired on us and our ship was hit. Freddie – Freddie died in the water with a thousand other men. The sea took him.'

I saw fire raining down over a dark sea. I saw a ship – a titanic city of metal – sinking into the cold, solemn swell of the ocean. I saw the grey waves swallowing a thousand burning bodies . . . And I saw it now – the sun high over the glittering, peaceful water. The ship was a dark skeleton on the seabed, resting, rusting, many miles from the sunlight – forgotten. A thousand lost boys were part of the beautiful blue ocean now. They were foam on the surface of the water.

We sat quietly for a while. Moth breathed in and out, in and out. I understood this moment. She had seen it now. She knew. She was wondering, perhaps, how her heart was still beating. Then: 'You survived.' She was proud.

David Stark nodded stiffly. 'The magazine exploded when we were first hit – I was caught in the flames. It was Freddie who got me out and pulled me on to the deck. That was the last time I saw him before the ship went down – everything was so confused . . . I jumped into the water, breaking both my legs. I would have drowned immediately, but I was picked up by a German torpedo boat. It wasn't known for some time that a few of us had been taken prisoner – my family thought I was dead until that Christmas. No matter how terrible it was in the camp, we told ourselves every day that we were the lucky ones. We were alive.'

Moth nodded. Her hands were pressed against her cheeks and tears ran through her pale fingers.

'I am alive because your son saved me,' David Stark said softly. 'Freddie was like a brother to me. If you ever need anything – anything at all, I will always be here to help you . . .'

Moth tried to make the words 'thank you' with her mouth, but no sound came out. She tried again: 'Thank you.' Then she looked at the silver fountain pen in her hands. 'I want you to keep this, David,' she whispered. She pressed the pen into his hand and gently folded his scarred fingers around it. 'It belongs to you now.'

49

Father took Mama to the London clinic that afternoon, and she came home to us three and a half weeks later. Doctor Berger had advised her to remain at the clinic for at least another month, but she was determined to return to us and he had relented, on the condition that she receive appropriate nursing care under his guidance. I hadn't asked yet, but I hoped, perhaps, that Moth might help us. She had been a Nightingale nurse once, after all.

The summer was all but over. Afternoons dissolved quickly into evenings; the sun, when it shone, was paler, a little lower in the sky. I was supposed to start at my new school in Norwich that very week, but Father made arrangements for me to remain at home until after the next holiday. He said I would have to do some extra work to catch up, and was rather surprised when I volunteered to take Latin lessons from dear Mr Pickersgill.

'But I thought you hated Latin,' he said.

I just shrugged.

'You're a mystery to me, Henry!' He laughed, shaking his head.

Father brought Mama home on a cool and blustery evening. She was sitting in the passenger seat of the motor car, wrapped up in the tartan motoring blanket. Father took her arm and led her to the front door where I stood waiting. Nanny Jane was upstairs, putting Piglet to bed. She had said Mama would not want to be too crowded by a big welcoming ceremony, so it had just been me, standing there for nearly an hour, shifting from one foot to another, waiting for the car to appear. Nanny Jane said I should wait in the study and look out of the window, but I said I wanted Mama to see me there as soon as she arrived.

She still looked thin and as fragile as a bird, but there was a little colour in her cheeks, and her beautiful eyes were no longer glazed, they were the eyes that I remembered — clear and wise. She put her arms around me and held me to her. I was frightened that she would smell of hospitals and doctors, but she didn't. She smelt of rose-water and a soothing, homely smell that I couldn't name. She smelt like my Mama.

We had a dreamy, quiet, sunlit breakfast together the next morning – Mama, Father, Nanny Jane, Piglet and me. The white tablecloth gleamed in the morning light; teaspoons tinkled prettily as they stirred teacups; Father's newspaper rustled and turned, rustled and turned. It was as if we were all pretending that a family breakfast like this was a perfectly usual occurrence. I drank up every blissful second of it.

I could see that Mama was stronger after her stay in hospital, or at least she was determined to be so. She poured the steaming tea steadily. She buttered her toast in smooth, sweeping strokes. *With Moth's help*, I thought, *she will soon be even stronger.*

The telephone rang then, and I got up. 'I'll get it, shall I, Father?' I said. He frowned and raised an eyebrow, but he didn't stop me.

It was Mr Pickersgill.

'Henrietta!' he said. 'Good news about Game-keeper's Cottage . . . It should be ready quite soon. There's not much in the way of structural work required. The roof is fixed already, and the windows have been replaced – David Stark has been the most tremendous help, I can't tell you!'

I was worried though. 'But are you absolutely sure that Moth – Mrs Young –doesn't want to come back home to Hope House?' I spoke quietly, aware of how strange my words would sound if Mama or Father should hear me.

'No,' he said. 'She says this will be a fresh start, somewhere peaceful.'

'Well – if she's sure . . .'

'Quite sure. Immovable in fact – you know what she's like . . .'

I smiled.

'And . . . I now have to try to explain something rather tricky to your father. Do you think you could put him on the line, please?'

Father came out of the dining room then, and I passed the pieces of the telephone to him.

'You're quite the early bird this morning, Truman,' Father said warmly. I was pleased that they were using each other's first names. For some reason, it made me feel proud.

'I see,' said Father. 'Well, I'm delighted that we can stay here at Hope House, of course, but . . . Yes, go on . . .' There was a long pause, during which Father slowly turned around to look at me, an expression of complete bewilderment on his face. 'A *gift*?' he said into the telephone. 'To Henrietta? The *house*? What on earth . . . ?' Another long pause. 'But – is it all quite . . . legal?' Father shook his head and sat down on the wooden bench beside the telephone table. 'Who . . . ?' he said. 'Why . . . ?' And then he laughed. 'Fine, fine! No, I'm not going to argue with you, Truman.' He laughed again, still shaking his head and gazing at me with that same bewildered expression. 'Well, yes – it's just . . . It's not exactly every day that one's daughter is given a house by a mysterious benefactor . . . Well, that would be lovely. Yes, why don't you come over and join us for dinner later this week so you can explain properly?'

I went to Nightingale Wood to meet Moth. I half hoped that Robert would appear, but somehow I knew that he wouldn't. I hadn't seen him for weeks now – not since the day I rescued Piglet from the Hardys . . . the day I brought Mama home from Helldon. I thought I saw something moving between the trees as I walked – the shimmer of honey-gold hair, but every time I turned to look at it, it vanished. I smiled, happy to let that flicker of sunlight dance elusively beside me. I didn't have to see it to know it was there.

I found Moth, and we walked together through the forest into Frith Meadow. We stopped for a moment to look at Gamekeeper's Cottage. I gazed through the new kitchen window and imagined Moth inside, sitting at the kitchen table. She was wearing a green dress instead of her usual tattered blankets. David Stark was sitting beside her. They were drinking tea, and he was reading to her from a book.

Moth and I walked across the fields towards the sea. She said there was something she wanted to do, for all those boys on Alfred's ship. It would be a sort of memorial, she said.

I looked at her as we walked. *Moth was a witch once*, I thought – and it was so strange to think of that first time I had seen her. *She was a character from a fairy tale, lost in the woods.* But now I understood who she really was. She was a mother, a friend, someone who had been broken and was putting herself back together. She was real.

It was a beautiful afternoon – the last truly warm day of the year. The sky was like a vast sheet of blue paper, thumb-smudged with chalk.

We walked through fields high with golden corn, down farm tracks, along bridle paths and across old bridges. We followed the river until it spilt, yawning, into the ocean. We stood together on a narrow point of land, a peninsula carved out by the allied forces of the river and the sea.

Moth had brought something with her: a wreath, woven with berries and rosehips and the last of the late poppies. She threw it now – where the silver-green of the river met the grey-blue sea. We watched the wreath bobbing like a brightly coloured buoy. It rose and fell with the waves, and I thought of ships and storms and adventures – *Treasure Island, The Little Mermaid, Peter Pan, Moonfleet* . . . I stood close, tucked against Moth's side.

The wreath was carried out to sea and we stood together and watched it until it disappeared.

'For all our lost boys,' Moth whispered.

I hoped the waves would carry Moth's message of remembrance far, far across the sea, to the place where Alfred's ship had sunk, and then further – through the long night, through a universe of sea and stars, all the way to Neverland.

50

Nanny Jane and Mrs Berry organized a picnic for us on the lawn that afternoon, to celebrate Mama's return. It was a wonderful spread – sandwiches, cakes, sausage rolls and the last strawberries of the year – better even than Piglet's tea party a few weeks before, because now we were all here together. While we waited for Mama and Father to join us, I jiggled Piglet on my lap, singing her a jolly song about ponies clip-clopping along.

We ate potted-meat sandwiches. Nanny Jane walked towards us, carrying a beautifully iced sponge cake with a pink candle in the centre.

'Happy un-birthday, Henry!' she said, handing it to me. And then, more sincerely: 'I really am so sorry I forgot.'

'It doesn't matter,' I said, gazing at the lovely surprise.

'It does,' she said.

'Yes,' I agreed. 'It does.' And I grinned.

Nanny Jane gave me a wink. 'There might even be one or two presents for you later on . . .'

Piglet reached out for the cake with her potted-meat-smeared hands.

'No, Piglet,' I said, gently, holding it out of her reach, 'Not yet.'

'Mm!' she said angrily. Then she stuffed a mangled bit of sandwich into her mouth with the flat of her hand.

I laughed, kissing her fluffy head.

Mama and Father came out into the garden at last. Mama was dressed warmly, with a peacock-blue shawl around her shoulders. Her hair was loose down her back. I thought that she had never looked more beautiful. Without thinking, I lifted Piglet up towards her as they approached, and then remembered with a jolt what Mama had said that night in the attic: she had never held the baby.

Mama hesitated for a moment, then took Piglet from me. Father looked on, his smile a little tight.

Don't cry, Piglet, I prayed silently. *Please don't cry.*

But Piglet was a reliable little soul.

'Ba!' she cried out happily, and touched Mama's

cheek with a small, sticky hand.

Mama's face was alight. It was as if she held the whole world in her arms. Her eyes shone and she kissed Piglet two, three, four times, holding her tightly.

'Hello,' she said, blinking back her tears and kissing her baby again. 'Hello, my little one.'

'Ba!' Piglet said, delighted.

Good old Piglet.

Mrs Berry brought out salmon sandwiches on the formal china — the rose-painted set we hardly ever used. She brought a glass of lemonade for me and crystal champagne saucers for Mama, Father and Nanny Jane.

'No point in all these pretty things sitting on the shelf gathering dust,' she said firmly. 'Welcome home, Mrs Abbott — and happy un-birthday to you, Miss Henrietta!'

And there was a toast.

A little later, as we lay on the rug, digesting the feast, Father said, 'We can't call the baby Piglet for ever, you know. Imagine the ragging she'll get at school.'

I laughed.

'But not Roberta,' I said.

There was a moment in which no one said anything at all.

'No. Not Roberta,' Father agreed.

'I mean,' I said, 'she just doesn't look like a Roberta.'

I looked into Mama's eyes and, through all the pain and all the sadness, I could see a new strength there. She looked steadily at the little creature sitting on her lap. 'No, she isn't a Roberta,' she said softly.

Father took the baby and held her up in front of him, looking into her huge eyes very seriously. 'What's your name, baby?'

Piglet chuckled and reached out to grab Father's nose. 'Babby!' she said, and we laughed.

'Bobbie,' I said, quite suddenly, surprising even myself.

Father looked at me, then back at Piglet. He inspected her face very closely. 'Is that who you are? Are you Bobbie?'

Piglet waved her spoon. 'Ba!' she said.

'Yes,' Mama said. 'Yes, yes, yes. Our bonny Bobbie.'

Bobbie beamed at her and held out her little fat arms.

Long after everyone else had gone back inside, I remained on the rug with Mama. We lay there next to each other, listening to the blackbird singing, feeling the air grow cooler on our skin. Church bells rang in the village.

It was that perfect moment of dusk – that rich, pink moment between day and night. I waited for the nightingale. I told Mama that Moth had taught me to whistle to him.

'I'm afraid he will have gone by now, Hen,' Mama said gently.

'Gone?'

'Away – for the winter. The nightingale is just a summer visitor. At this very moment, he will be stretching out his little wings in a warm African sunset.'

I thought about this, trying to imagine our nightingale so far away. It made me sad to think that he had another home, another place that belonged to him that had nothing to do with me or Moth or the woods of Hope House.

'Next summer,' I said. 'He'll come back next summer and we will go to Nightingale Wood together and listen to him singing.'

'Next summer,' Mama promised.

'It's magical, Mama,' I whispered. 'The whole forest fills with silver light and then, quite suddenly, you're floating with the nightingale's song up in the stars.'

Mama was quiet for a moment and then she said, 'What a wonderful place the world would be, Hen, if everyone had your imagination.'

The sun dipped lower and I thought I saw the first star of the evening – a pinprick of light directly above us. There was a fluttering movement in the grass next to me and I turned my head to look. It was a moth. Its fragile wings were the most extraordinary colour – a dusty, mottled gold. It was so beautiful – I turned to see if Mama had seen it too. But Mama wasn't looking at the moth, she was looking at me, and her eyes were shining with tears. 'I'm not out of the woods yet, Hen,' she said in a low voice. 'I'm still – a little lost.'

'I know. But it's going to be all right, Mama,' I said. 'We've found you now.' And I thought of that little phrase Mr Berry had taught me – the motto of Paris: *'Fluctuat nec mergitur.'*

She blinked.

'It's Latin, Mama,' I said, and something twisted inside my chest.

She sobbed a little laugh – 'Yes . . .'

'She is tossed by the waves but she does not sink.'

Mama couldn't say anything at all for a moment. She just took my hand and held it very tightly. I thought I might never let go.

'She does not sink, Hen,' Mama whispered at last. 'She does not sink.'

The moth fluttered again and this time Mama saw it too. It waited for a moment, as if gathering strength, and then it took off. We watched as it flew higher and higher. Its wings caught the last rays of the sun and then, just for a second, it was a flame – a tiny flutter of gold in defiance of the dying light.

Acknowledgements

Heartfelt thanks to my editor Rachel Leyshon for her wisdom, vision, patience and inspiration. I am so grateful to her and to the legend that is Barry Cunningham for having faith in me (and, more importantly, in Hen) right from the start. Thanks also to the rest of the amazing Chicken House team – particularly Laura Myers, Rachel Hickman, Elinor Bagenal, Jazz Bartlett and Kesia Lupo. Thanks to my fabulous copy-editor and proofreader for their eagle eyes, and to Studio Helen for creating such a beautiful cover: I cried when I saw the first drawing because it was just so perfect.

This book began with Luigi and Alison Bonomi and the Montegrappa First Fiction Prize. *The Secret of Nightingale Wood* wouldn't exist if they hadn't picked my manuscript from the pile. Huge thanks to both of them for all their warmth, hard work and unwavering support. Thanks also to Yvette Judge and Isobel Abulhoul at the Emirates Festival of Literature for making me feel like a proper writer from the very start.

I shall be forever in debt to Rachel Hamilton for saving my bacon with her insight and reassurance during several cutting crises, and thank you to Emily Steel and Paul Skinner for sharing their honest, writerly perspectives when I couldn't see the Nightingale Wood for the trees.

Thank you to my husband and best friend Iain Martin for being such an encouraging early reader, for always telling me when I'm overthinking things, and for trying not to sing Guns N' Roses too loudly when I'm editing. Thanks to the wonderful Stacy Donne without whom I would have been utterly lost on many an occasion. I am deeply and eternally grateful for the friendship of the beautiful and wise Louise Milner-Moore. Big, big thanks and buckets of love to Bronwen, Tom, Jeannine, Jen and all my other dear, dear friends, teaching colleagues, early readers, fellow writers and students – too numerous to mention here – for being so kind and so supportive of my writing.

Enormous hugs of gratitude to Mum and Dad for so many things, including reading to me when I was little and bringing me up in a house full of books. Thank you for putting up with all the exhausted grumpiness of a grown-up boomerang daughter who is always trying to do far too much at once. Ooh – and a belated thank you for those audiobook cassettes of *Alice's Adventures in Wonderland, The Secret Garden* and *The Jungle Book* – I listened to them so many times when I was small that the stories must have soaked into my brain as I slept; *The Secret of Nightingale Wood* owes so much to these beautiful, classic tales. Thanks to my brothers Will and Pete Strange for being proud of me, for sage advice and for laughter along the way.

Lastly, thanks go to our little furry twit, Maddy Cat, and to our own bright star, Axl.

*

The Secret of Nightingale Wood is being published in 2016, the 100th anniversary of The Battle of the Somme and The Battle of Jutland. It seems fitting to end this book by remembering all those who gave their lives in the First World War.